ROBERT PHILLIPS

J. M. DeSantis

ROBERT PHILLIPS

J. M. DeSantis

Dark Fire Press
New Jersey, USA

For

HPL, REH, AS, and JRRT

About the Book

Originally published in 1943, this book did not see wide circulation and was considered lost shortly after the Second World War. Black Raven Publishing House burned down in January of 1947, with nearly all of its published works, including this one which it would appear sold very few copies. (No doubt contemporary minds were more focused on the War in Europe and its aftermath.) A fair copy was recently rediscovered and is reprinted here in its original form, with all included notes (by BRPH) and letters from the original 1943 edition.

The publisher is indebted to J. M. DeSantis for this discovery and his permission to use his copy to republish the haunting words of Prof. J. Lewis. Thanks also to Susan P. DeSantis, Edmond A. DeSantis, and K. L. Young for their assistance thereof.

The book's funding and publication were made possible by The Patreon Fund, under the care of Messrs. Dwayne Farver, Jakub Kowal, Jeff Stoner, Hakan Tandogan, and Ian Sniffen. We thank them humbly for their immense and patient support.

The Account of Robert Phillips

From the papers of former Harvard
Professor John Lewis

John Ambrose Lewis

1943
Black Raven Publishing House

Providence, Rhode Island
United States of America

Prologue

It is with a considerable amount of apprehension that I so much as recall the tale of Robert Phillips, even so many years after his disappearance—despite what the authorities say on the matter.

The reasons for such feelings have nothing whatever to do with the man named here. For a good portion of the time I knew him, Robert was well-reasoning and kind, even if eccentric. Even after that strange madness seemed to take hold of him, I still felt nothing but amiably toward and genuinely concerned for my friend.

Rather it is the very nature of his disappearance, the events which led up to it, the horrifying thing I believe that I witnessed, and the hideous truths I have since learned, which has driven me to the sorry state I now find myself in: no longer a respected professor of History and searching obsessively for any remaining copy of an old and forbidden grimoire in order that I might destroy it, and being hunted unceasingly by members of the cults who follow the teachings of an ancient visionary named Abdul Alhazred.

Despite my passionate and determined course, I fear that in the end, I shall not succeed, so frighteningly fanatical and wide-spread, albeit secretive, are the influences of those Nameless Cults described in the work of Von Junzt. I even begin to worry that they've men on the faculties of Harvard and Miskatonic, and abroad I'm afraid the mad ravings of an unhinged and disgraced American historian are not taken seriously. Then there were the copies Robert acquired and his work which were never found.

But that there are copies in Argentina, France, and Great Britain (and those are just the ones I am able to confirm), information about Alhazred and his book in the New York Library, an unconfirmed and lost copy of the hideous grimoire in California are enough to confirm that these cults have spread beyond the borders of the Miskatonic River Valley—and indeed they did not even originate there. Then there is the fact that I believe the cultists are closing in on me, despite my nomadic and largely anonymous existence since leaving Harvard and even Massachusetts behind me forever.

What I am here about to confess in detail you will not find much information to corroborate, I fear. The cultists have done their work, and officially it is the accepted position that Robert Phillips moved to Italy some three years ago, despite the absence of other evidence which would confirm that story to hold true. No missing persons report has been filed, and there is no further investigation into the case. In fact, there is no case at all.

Other vague references to cases of about a decade or so before this writing are confirmable to those who do research of their own. I would urge the reader be careful in that research. If they must look further, the disappearances of a Massachusetts artist named Pickman[1], a man from Vermont

---

1   Richard Upton Pickman was a renowned Boston

named Akeley, many of the locals of a little known town named Innsmouth (outside of the Miskatonic Valley), and a sinister man named Whateley all will lend further credibility to my tale.

That said, I beg you not discredit Robert's story, no matter how weird or seemingly impossible the implications. I swear by any sanity and dignity that I have left that the whole of it is completely true. I am still an historian above all things, and uncovering the truth is ever the principle value of mine.

At the very least, hold all judgment until the bitter end and all the facts are laid bare. Then when you find yourself drawing your own conclusions, even should you find me to be completely mad, I implore you not delve into hidden and darksome things. There are realities within this world which men should rightfully fear even the barest knowledge of, and if you find yourself presented with a translated copy of a book known as *Al-Azif* or *The Necronomicon*, I beg you not to crack open even the cover of the tome and throw it into the fire as soon as you are alone.

In truth I myself have questioned if what I saw in the end were not a mere hallucination or some trick the lights played that night in the old Phillips Manor, yet I cannot, in good faith, ignore how disturbing and real the incident had been at the time, nor what it all but confirmed, not least based upon my experiences with Robert leading up to that horrible night and confirmed by the research I've done since.

Though, perhaps I get ahead of myself. It would

---

artist, well known for his macabre paintings and who inexplicably disappeared in 1926.

be best to begin my tale with how and when I met Robert, for it will give you a point of reference for how the character of this man of such great potential changed, and to give a clear and stark point of reference before the beginning of my good friend's slow spiral toward his undoing.

It may seem pedantic and trivial, but I wish to describe the full scope of my dealings with Robert. I will attempt to give no conjecture as to events, save for my own feelings at the time. After all, I am an historian by trade, and I wish to give whoever you are who is reading this the barest facts of the case as they were.

Because of the nature of my relationship with Robert, I offer this manuscript in two parts. The first being firsthand accounts of my interactions with Robert whilst we were both students at Miskatonic University, much written from memory, though a few scenes are directly quoted from the journals I kept between 1931 and 1936, each account written at or about the time of the incidents (and which, as of this writing, I still have in my possession)[2].

The second half is largely made up of correspondences with Robert, with very few encounters. Where a complete letter is referenced (all twenty-two of them included with this manuscript, and in ascending order of their dates), I will refer to them by the dates in which Robert wrote them and the numbers which I have added to them that they might more easily be referenced and kept in a

---

2   These journals were never found and were not among the papers of Professor Lewis, else select readings might have been appended to this text.

certain order[3]. I have no carbon copies of my own letters to Robert.

That said, let us begin.

JAL

---

3   Because of the nature of this publication, and for the ease of the reader, the editor has included the letters from Robert Phillips directly in the pages at the point of Professor J. Lewis's references, and removed Lewis's written references to the letters' numbers and dates. As for Prof. Lewis's own letters to Mr. Phillips, any attempt to locate them have come up empty and the publisher can only surmise, like the journals (see note 2), they are unrecoverable.

Part I: Miskatonic University

I

It was in the first term of our second year at university when I was introduced to Robert Phillips. We were both studying History at Miskatonic University in Arkham, Massachusetts, and I had already heard rumours about the illustrious promise of this astounding genius. Our specific areas of study were slightly different, however I asked a mutual friend, Ashton, for an introduction. Ashton was all too happy to oblige having nothing but the utmost respect for Robert and having the sense Robert would like me. So when the opportunity came, Ashton invited me to a small gathering where Robert was expected to be.

I cannot say that I was not intimidated. So much did this fellow student's reputation as an immensely intelligent and capable historian and linguist precede him, that I felt my hands clam up upon entering the room. But that all fell away in an instant, as Robert smiled at me and said:

"Ah! John Lewis. Or is it Lewis John? I can't keep it straight."

"Am I to understand your name is Phillips, then?" I retorted, with a wry smile of my own.

"Our mothers were unkind to us," said Robert, extending his hand, his smile never wavering. "I'm afraid future students will not know how to references us in the card catalog when finally we've been published."

Not very witty I'm afraid, but the two of us had a good laugh, and right there, from one little commonality, we fell into conversation and became fast friends. "Thick as thieves" is the way many of our peers described us, though despite the fact that we had two first names and a love for history, the two of us could not be any more different.

Where Robert was lively and always moving and shifting, I was calm, quiet, and consistent. But that only seemed to endear us to one another. I think unconsciously, I was always looking for more adventure, and Robert needed something stable in his life. Though to suggest Robert was unstable is unfair. Rather he was full of life and energy, and so quick witted. I never thought myself a dumb man, but next to Robert I was practically a Neanderthal.

More, Robert was from Arkham. His family had an estate in the French Hill district, whereas I was a complete outsider, having traveled to Arkham all the way from California. That may indeed seem strange, but I had read the works of Dr. Ferdinand C. Ashley, and had gone through school with the idea of becoming an expert in the field of Ancient History just as he was himself. So, when I learned that he was a professor at Miskatonic, I wanted nothing else but to attend school in Arkham and hopefully study under the man.

My proposed area of expertise was in the interconnected relations between Egypt and Rome, and this led to further topics of conversation between Robert and I, as we were both fluent in Latin. I preferred to research from direct sources whenever possible and so knowing the language was paramount, but Robert's fluency was simply because he was deeply interested in the Linguistic histories of Ancient cultures and their beliefs. But to limit Robert in such a way is also unfair.

By the time we met, Robert was already fluent in Latin, Greek, and French, and had solid reading comprehension of at least two other languages. He had read *Bulfinch's Mythology* at the age of ten, and could quote whole passages of *The Iliad* and *The Odyssey* from memory, without pause, both from Pope's translation and the original Greek.

Naturally, his long-standing mastery of Ancient Greek and Latin and font of knowledge concerning all of the myths of the Ancient Greeks and the Romans led him to pursue new frontiers once at Miskatonic University. He turned his attention to the near Middle East and its more ancient myths and languages.

Yet despite Robert's fixed area of study, he read widely and without any sort of pretense or prejudice. Be it a paper on the finer points of the circulatory system from one of Professor Morgan's classes or a copy of *Ranch Romances*, Robert read voraciously and with such a keen attention to detail, even at the great speed with which he consumed the written word.

I found it incredible—and even a little intimidating—that a man could recall so clearly the details of everything he read, even months later. More than once I saw him in one of his quieter moods, whilst we visited friends around the campus, pull a book off of a shelf and read it cover to cover in a matter of hours. And I had a fine time watching him prove that he had indeed absorbed every detail of what he read to those who still did not know him well and deigned to challenge his lofty claims. But it was always in good fun.

Robert Phillips was an absolute genius, and a good-natured one. When his immense knowledge came flowing out, even in the most pompous and contradictory of moments, it was difficult not to forgive him at once. He was a league ahead of us all, and so any friendly competition was not aimed at Robert.

But as I said, I never saw it go to his head. He never spoke in a condescending tone. He was always quick to offer his opinion or assistance whenever it was asked for. And he always gave credit and praise whenever and wherever it was due. I cannot deny I was absolutely in awe of the man, as this writing may suggest. Remembering now how he was then brings a smile to my face and verily my eyes tear up. It is so difficult a thing to recall those days.

I think the tragedy of his fall was felt hardest by the University itself, for the professors, though indeed they liked Robert (what wasn't to like?), I think more saw a ray of hope in him and his success at the college and beyond. He was their golden child, as it were.

Robert came from solid Massachusetts stock on both his parents' sides, his ancestors having lived in the region of the Miskatonic Valley since it was first settled. Whether by blood or marriage, his line could be traced back to nearly all of the old families of the area, yet he shewed none of their peculiar fascinations with the occult or other macabre dealings that many of those tied to the region did.

His parents had been long dead, and left Robert with a considerable inheritance and their mansion in Arkham. Though he had no personal relationships with any of his extended family, and certainly knew the opinions of some regarding them, he was proud of his heritage nonetheless. I think the college was even more so, considering its history.

Only a few years before our enrollment and through much of the 1920s, the school had suffered a series of unfortunate events. Stories floated around campus that one of their best medical students suffered from the most insane preoccupations with reanimating the dead, the association with which many believed to have led to the school's own Dr. Allen Halsey being locked away in an asylum, before his and the former student's disappearance[1].

Then there were the vague rumours about the school's Special Collections and dramatic events surrounding said collection. Only now do I know the reasons for Dr. Armitage's seeming hostility toward Robert and the deeper truths about his earlier dealings with a thing by the name of Whateley. It is no wonder he retired from his post as Chief Librarian.

There was a sense that the Miskatonic staff felt

---

1   Records show Dr. Allen Halsey was in fact committed to Sefton Asylum in 1905. Likely Prof. Lewis here refers to Miskatonic University Medical graduate, Dr. Herbert West. Canadian war records list a Dr. H. West as being a surgeon in the Canadian army in 1915 during World War I, but most of West's post-Miskatonic career is quite obscure. If the rumours are to be believed, Dr. Halsey did indeed go missing from the asylum in 1921, and was never after found.

Robert's destiny for greatness would restore their good name and good standing and put to rest the incessant rumours and bogey tales that seemed to surround the University, its history, and the history of the surrounding area. Naturally their insistence on secrecy led many of us to delve further into the stories (we were there for studying and academics after all), but we came up with little, and Robert would always laugh us off.

Strange, unworldly gods, worshiped by cults in the surrounding towns. Criminal activity in Dunwich and Innsmouth. There were even rumours of a strange, aquatic look which the natives of that latter town possessed. "The Innsmouth Look" it was called. We'd often question Robert about these things, but he'd merely chuckle and tell us the stories were no more real than the claims against innocent women who were burned as witches in nearby Salem—ancient fears given a new face in the mythless New World, perverted by Puritanical "wisdom". They were things to be studied and enjoyed (in a manner of speaking), but he reminded us that our own studies were much more important.

How right he was and wise that advice. If only he had heeded it fully himself. But who could have then known the accursed history of the Miskatonic Valley had wound its way from the very cultures Robert studied? Perhaps the old families and the college are cursed indeed.

II

It was sometime before the summer of our third year that Robert first came upon those strange and seemingly nonsensical words and the Mad Arab who wrote them which went on to become an obsession of his for the remainder of his tragic life.

We were in the Miskatonic Library looking over books in preparation for the end of term exams. Robert at that time had grown weary of the long hours of study (and as usual, was well ahead of the rest of us). So for fun he sat down with a copy of *Deorum Mundo* by Claudus Insapiens[1]. As I said, Robert would read just about anything, and likely he did so because it was truly to have a light-hearted break from serious study.

I barely took notice of his leaving the table where we both sat or that he returned with said book. Nor did it register the strange seeming gibberish he was mumbling to himself again and again, before he uttered the word, Nyarlathotep.

"What's that, Robert?" said I.

---

1   That book and Insapiens himself, it would seem, were so lauded by the academic community that one cannot even find a copy of it in print anymore, except in very special collections of certain libraries, and only as a piece of publication history, not as a serious work to study.

Then he uttered the name again. *Nyarlatho-tep*. "Have you heard of him, John?" Indeed I had heard the name before, but rather than the dread it should have filled me with, I merely returned:

"It's not a pharaoh in the List of Kings," said I. "And I'm not so familiar with the lesser men of Egypt."

"He was not a pharaoh," said Robert. "It says here that he 'traveled into Greece sometime between 800 and 900 A.D. and brought with him the words of the Mad Arab, Abdul Alhazred.'"

I titled my head to one side, taking my glasses off and looked him square in the face. Robert continued on, doing his best to pronounce the words:

"Fuhn-gloo-ee mmm-gloo nahf K'thoo-loo Rily-eah wagah nahgl fuh-tahgn."

My brow furrowed.

"It's strange," said Robert, "I don't know if that's right."

Robert turned the book to me and pointed to the passage in question. The words written in the Greek Alphabet read:

Πη'νγλθι μγλω'ναφη Cτηθλɳθ Ρ'λυεη ωγαη'ναγλ
φηταγν

Or, in its English transliteration: *Ph'nglui mglw'nafh Cthulhu R'lyeh wgah'nagl fhtagn.*

"Well it's not Greek."

"Don't I know it. Nor is it Latin. Nor Arabic. Nor any language I can think it might be. It's almost unutterable gibberish. And that name. Abdul Alhazred."

I continued to puzzle over the words and began to turn the page. Robert continued.

"It is not a traditional Arabic name. The double "ul" is highly irregular. Impossible. And even the book it mentions. In Arabic the name is said to be *Al-Azif.* But that too is a strange word. *Azif.*[2]"

As he continued, I turned over the book.

"Oh, Robert, really. Insapiens? The man likely made the whole thing up." Insapiens was known, among scholars, to have infamously written at great length such claims as that in the Far East, around present day Japan, there was worshiped a Sun God called Guin Fulgur Sapientes.

"Indeed I'd say so, Lewis, but for the odd name there. Cthulhu, sometimes pronounced Kloo-loo."

"I've never heard it. Certainly nothing written about in the Egyptian texts I've read."

"Nor in the Latin texts either of us have come across, or in the Arabic I've perused. But those folktales you all are always pestering me about, well, Cthulhu is a name that has come up in some of those. Some demon of sorts said to cannibalise men in their sleep, I think."

I looked puzzled at him for a moment.

"I know what I've always said about those stories, John, but it is so odd, isn't it?"

"Well, if the people who pass those stories

---

2   For those readers unfamiliar with Arabic and naming conventions therein, Phillips's claim here is quite true. The publisher's limited investigation into this has turned up that there have been many arguments in certain circles about the name Abdul Alhazred and whether or not the name was poorly translated or was used to help obscure The Mad Arab and the things he is purported to have found. Some have argued Insapiens himself could be a culprit for the mistranslation, but Insapiens lived around 1010 A.D., sixty years after the book is said to have been first translated.

around still are as ignorant as you claim," said I with a smile, "Insapiens would be a fair source for such ludicrousness."

"True," Robert shifted his eyes downward for a moment. "I'm not saying anything for certain, John, but what if those stories are left over from some sort of ancient cult from the Middle East?." A smile spread across Robert's lips, and his eyes grew a little wide in that manic way that was his habit when he seemed positively glued to an idea. "What an adventure that would be. To peruse the texts of a heretofore largely unknown religion and one that somehow found its way to Arkham."

By that look, I could see there was no further talking to Robert at the moment about it. He was going to obsess over it for some hours still. As I dove back into a history on the Nabataean Kings, I could hear Robert repeating the strange words to himself and the name Alhazred, as though by chanting them he would learn the truth.

I caught up with Robert the following afternoon after my Economics class. I hated math, but I figured I might as well learn one which might be applicable to my studies. I found Robert in his room, pacing the floor and mumbling the same strange words I had left him puzzling over in the Library the night before. I thought he did not even notice my entrance and was about to speak when he suddenly uttered, not stopping for a moment in his pacing:

"Armitage is a fool." I'd never heard Robert speak poorly of anyone, unless in jest, and I'd never seen him agitated. I sat down on the bed.

"I spent much of the night in the Library trying to find other sources on Alhazred and his *Al-Azif*.

Even Cthulhu and that strange language. There was nothing there that I could find. Dr. Armitage was burning the midnight oil, compiling a new reference sheet for the freshmen arriving in the fall. So I brought the Insapiens book to him."

He paused. His eyes were wide as he paced, hands at his side, gaze floor-ward. I waited. Robert could indeed get moody at times, but typically he was more pensive. I always felt it best not to interrupt him and let him come out with it himself. After a few more short laps back and forth, he said:

"I've never seen a learned man behave so ridiculously." He continued to pace, continued to look downward. "It was like I had slapped him in the face. He staggered, Lewis, actually staggered. Like some actor in a Chaplin reel."

His pacing became a bit faster. His eyes darted back and forth. They reddened. I'd never seen him in such a state.

"Then all of a sudden, such a purple rage came out of him. He ripped the book from my hand and began to laugh, but there was no mirth in it. He said the book was supposed to be removed from the shelves on account of Insapiens's unreliability. But I pressed, not hard. Only as a learned man might argue his point. I swear I thought the man was going to slap me in earnest then.

"'Grow up, Mr. Phillips,' he said to me. 'You'll have no career in Linguistics or anywhere in Academia if you determine to use Insapiens as a source of anything resembling knowledge.' But I could not help it. I uttered the name *Al-Azif* and then the purple and all other colour completely left his face.

"'Child!' his voice cracked. 'I'm so disappointed

in you, Phillips. You had such promise!' And then he stormed off."

I looked at Robert. He looked as though he had been slapped, and his face even turned a slight shade of pink. He was wounded. Insulted. I could tell.

"I don't understand it. Dr. Armitage could have at least heard me out. Whatever the source, those legends are spoken of here in the Miskatonic Valley."

"Perhaps Insapiens is the source of the legend, and it merely ends there."

"Oh come now, John. You know that's not how myth and folklore work. And Armitage's behaviour was so strange."

"I'll agree with you there, Robert," said I. I recall sighing then. I could see he was so agitated. "Why don't we go out for a bit? Perhaps a little air would do you well?"

Robert did not respond. He just continued to pace, eyes wide.

"Robert?"

"Just leave me be, Lewis! I need to think! Can't you see that?!"

It was the first time I'd ever seen Robert snap at anyone, and at me of all people. I knew he was upset, his ego bruised by Dr. Armitage's words, but his outburst cut deep nonetheless. I quietly rose from the bed and left the room, closing the door behind me. Robert was still deep in thought and pacing back and forth across his room.

III

Not less than a few hours after the scene in his room, Robert caught up with me and apologised. He tried to explain that he had never been treated so harshly by anyone, and he was afraid he had turned the same behaviour on me. I brushed it off and reassured him that sometimes the anger has to go somewhere. Better me than a faculty member. That at least made him chuckle a bit.

The remainder of the term went without another outburst or direct incident. After all, we were deep into exams week and hadn't the time for much but earnest study. With any free time we had, even us erudite and scholarly students needed to unwind and take a break from our musty, book-filled haunts.

I noted on at least three occasions during that week that in very short, quiet moments, Robert looked with a faraway glance, as he muttered silently some words to himself. His moods, even his energetic ones, seemed tinged with some underlying and indecipherable emotion. I thought perhaps it was a bit of melancholy over his unfortunate and uncalled for scolding by Dr. Armitage, but I tried to make nothing of it.

After the exams, Robert seemed to be back to his normal self. We spent a bit of time on campus, visiting friends and taking a small respite from studies as we awaited the results from our exams. Robert had high marks again, though curiously he was not at the top of every class. In Linguistics in particular he was third on the list. Though a completely new development, I feared that agitated state might return, but Robert seemed unaffected by his placement in the ranks.

"You can't win 'em all, John," I recall were Robert's words, and he shook hands with Williams and Ashton who achieved first and second in the class, respectively. That was so much more like him.

That summer, Robert and I planned a trip to New York City for a week to see the new Empire State Building[1]. There we continued our studies, already thinking about our dissertations and what we were to spend the remainder of our studies working toward. Whilst there, we could not help but stop in at The New York Public Library and visit its collection, and the illustrious reading room on the third floor.

We planned to spend an entire day there (though it was hardly enough), seeking out what rare finds were not to be found in the Massachusetts area. It didn't matter to us if the work had anything to do with our areas of study or not. We merely wished to absorb whatever knowledge we could, not knowing when we might find ourselves in the position to visit New York again.

To that end, we split up at times to see what

---

1   The Empire State Building was completed in November of 1930, but was not opened to the public until May 1931, so by those standards, the building would be considered "new".

we could gather in different areas. I was taking a moment to admire a display the library had set up when Robert suddenly came around a corner. He looked agitated again, much more so than he had been that afternoon in the dormitory. My heart unwittingly sank and turned in my stomach.

"He lied!" A few people looked up from their books and in our direction. "Armitage lied!"

Someone hissed for silence. Robert came right up to me. He had a small, staple-bound book in his hand.

"Robert, please, keep it down." My eyes shifted to one side, and I noted there were quite a few of the library's occupants scowling at us. Robert opened the book in front of me and pointed to a passage near the middle of the right hand page.

The book was a hideous thing, filled with illustrations. Though crudely drawn, there was something about them that filled me with an unsettling sense of dread.

"Look here, John."

I did, though I was having trouble not returning my glance to the amateur sketch of some oddly anthropomorphic creature made up of different parts of animals, though unlike a sphinx, it was all blasphemously aquatic in nature, with a multitude of large, bulbous black eyes. I cannot say why, but even in the light of the day-lit New York Library a chill ran up my spine.

I turned my glance away and to the passage Robert was pointing to. There were written strange names which I had never before heard, but I shall certainly never forget: Yog-Sothoth and the corpse city of sunken R'lyeh. Included there too were Dagon, Cthulhu, and Abdul Alhazred.

I looked up at Robert, and I can recall distinctly that that was when I began to first question his mental health. (There was even a note I'd written about it in my journal when we came back from New York.) There was a look of mania in his eyes that I recognised. I had seen that look many times before when visiting my uncle who had been committed to an asylum when I was twelve. My mother and him had been so close before then.

"Where did you find this, Robert?" was all I could ask.

"I asked one of the librarians here about this book, and he pointed me to another man who told me that he read of Alhazred in a history on the Umayyad Caliphate. He was known as "The Mad Arab" because of his strange hallucinations later in his life, and having written a book about these visions while living in Damascus.

"That book, of course, is *Al-Azif*. It says here that the title *Al-Azif* is a rough translation of the 'nocturnal sound supposed to be the howling of demons', but that today it is more commonly known as *The Necronomicon*, a title given to it by Theodorus Philetas.

"Documented Latin translations of that book still exist, and a few are kept at libraries in the Americas and Europe. One of those libraries is Miskatonic!"

His voice began to rise again. People began to look at us once more.

"Miskatonic University has a copy of *Al-Azif!* Armitage knows it, and he's keeping it from me!"

A good number of people were beginning to stare. Robert went on at length, but I have no record of what he said. I recall it being something to the effect of accusations toward Arimtage and the University in general. I didn't pay much attention to the words he was saying. I could see he was in a frenzy, and my concern was for my friend and attempting to calm him. I knew he could not be thinking straight in the state he was in.

During that scene, two men walked toward us and we were asked to leave. Robert grew angry with them, but somehow I was able to lead him out, my heart racing all the while. So much then for the day at the New York Public Library.

A few hours later, whilst taking a walk through Central Park (which was notably not as impressive as the library), Robert apologised for his behaviour for the second time. I of course forgave him. He said he had just become so enraged that Dr. Armirage had treated him so horribly and insultingly, and yet there was the book, sitting in the Miskatonic Library the whole while. He seemed to be calm, so I ventured the question once more.

"Where did you find that book, Robert?"

"It was in with some filed away books on the upstairs floor," said he, sort of faraway and shaking his head. "It was apparently written by a man who used to donate to the Library some fifty years ago."

I smiled despite the fact of it being such an obscure source. Robert really had an uncanny knack for research and a keen mind. He literally could find a needle in a haystack.

"A self-published pamphlet?" was what I said to him, however. "Oh, Robert. Really."

"I know, John. I know," said Robert. "But there is something strange about the whole business."

"I agree."

"That book came out of the Middle East, went to Greece and was translated, then later it was translated into Latin."

I began to see where his calm mind was going with this. Robert had such a mind.

"That name. Abdul Alhazred. It must be some corrupted form of an Arabic original. And if the name was corrupted over time, you know as well as I that the text had to be." Then he whispered, almost to himself, "An entire lost culture and ancient belief system. It found its way into the Miskatonic Valley, and no one is studying it."

I looked at him. Robert was staring off into nothingness, but there was nothing of the mania I saw in his eyes earlier or in his dormitory room that day. This was Robert as I knew him: brilliant, confident, and thorough, the wheels in his mind turning as he worked out the problem. I gave him my silence and smiled again.

"I need to see that book, John. When we get back to Arkham, I'll approach Professor Rice about the matter."

"All right, Robert. All right."

And that was the end of it again for a while.

IV

The scene with Professor Rice—for so it can only be called—was not any less disturbing than that which Robert found himself in with Dr. Armitage during the previous semester. I was not there for the incident, just as I had been absent from the first, but between Robert's own account of that afternoon (once he had calmed down enough to speak clearly about it) and based on the corroboration of witnesses to the end of Robert's meeting with Professor Rice, I can confidently attest to that which I am about to tell.

We had been no more than two weeks back, and after his morning classes on Wednesday, Robert went directly to Professor Rice's office. Robert made his case, stating what he had found in the book by Claudus Insapiens, the evidence found in New York, and that with his knowledge of Arabic and Alhazred's own peculiar name, he theorised it very likely *The Necronomicon* suffered from many unfortunate translation errors.

According to Robert's report, he did not tell Professor Rice the entire story of his interaction with Dr. Armitage, but he did intimate that the head Librarian was "vehemently unwilling" to grant Robert access to *The Necronomicon*. He hoped, Robert said, that considering the book's value to the university and the area of the Miskatonic Valley, and Robert's own roots there, never mind his intentions, knowledge, and abilities, that Professor Rice would appeal to Armitage and allow Robert to see the book for himself and learn what he might. After all, wouldn't the university wish to have as accurate a translation as possible for such a rare find in their prized collection?

In retrospect, Robert stated that he did notice Professor Rice was fidgeting, pacing about, sitting and standing, and shifting things on his desk while Robert made his case. To Rice's credit, he did not interrupt Robert once, until the very end, and at least seemingly heard Robert out. But about the time that Robert asked for the appeal and access to the infamous book is when Professor Rice lost all composure.

He rose from his desk and started to yell at Robert at the top of his lungs, calling him a foolish, immature little boy. He threw Robert out of his office, marching toward the door and yelling into the hallway at Robert. Quite a few students were there to witness the scene, and Ashton said it was "quite unlike old iron-grey Rice to act in such a way".

Then with additional uncharacteristic violence, Professor Rice slammed the door on Robert, but not before yelling for all in hearing distance that Robert was a disappointment to his lineage and the institution, and if he continued in such a manner the only appeal being made would be to the dean about him being thrown out of the school. It was a wild overreaction, Robert knew that, but he was still red in the face from anger and embarrassment when I caught up with him.

"They are trying to hold me back, John," Robert said through gritted teeth. "They know my genius, and they want to keep me down so I don't out do them. Likely Rice and Armitage are attempting a translation of their own, or I brought it to their attention and like all learned and vain men they want the credit for themselves."

"That's a bit of a stretch, Robert, don't you think?" I said.

"Is it, John?!" and Robert turned on me with reddened eyes. They weren't clear, I could see. I'm not even certain if, in that moment, he saw his friend or rather just another enemy.

"Here is an obscure piece of Ancient History, a book the University keeps under lock and key, and I may have stumbled on a plausible hypothesis about the book, one that could perhaps shine light on much of our understanding not only of the Ancient Middle East, but the history of the founding of the Miskatonic Valley. And who better than Robert Phillips to achieve that? I who have deep roots in this country!

"They shame me and they censor me, John. They do not wish me to succeed. I have out done them and in their pride they wish to silence me before I rise too high."

"Robert," I ventured cautiously, not wishing to work him up any further than he already was, "I do agree that they are acting strangely about this, but perhaps there is another reason—"

"There is no other reason!" Robert screeched. "Are you going to throw in with them then?"

I straightened and went white. I had no idea what to say.

"Get out! Get out of here and leave me be!"

Without a word I rose and closed the door behind me. My heart broke to hear Robert sobbing on the other side of the door, but for the moment, I couldn't risk another outburst. It was three days before I saw Robert again, and he apologised to me. But after that incident I was even more careful with my words around him regardless of the man's mood—which also after that incident grew alarmingly unstable.

For the remainder of the term, we all saw little of Robert. He took to spending large amounts of time in his room and rarely shewed his face in class or even on campus during the day. Once or twice I called at his room, but Robert in one instance did not answer, and in the other he sent me away stating that he was grossly overtired and needed to sleep. There were rumours spread by those who kept late hours who claimed they saw Robert leaving campus or in the town of Arkham, seemingly walking in a single-minded way toward some unknown destination. To the credit of these rumours, whether it was in class during the day, answering his door, or in the middle of the night, Robert looked to be in a perpetually tired and haggard state. Though he and I were on good terms, even I knew little of his comings and goings.

It was just after the midterm exams that I finally caught up with him again. He had managed to make it to all of his exams, and he looked generally rested, but there were dark circles around his eyes and they shifted a bit as we spoke.

It was something of a strange run in. I don't think Robert expected to see me. I just sort of bumped into him leaving one exam. I expressed concern—carefully—but Robert dismissed my feelings, stating that he was just fine, that he was merely tired from all of the late hours. Half uncertainly, I decided to venture a question about the long hours.

"I'm not the first man they did this to, John," said Robert, and there was a cold simmering look in his eyes. Robert must have read the confusion in my expression. He continued without a word's encouragement from me. "There was a man named Whateley who had asked about the book about four or so years ago. I wasn't able to get much information, but Armitage was at the heart of it. Some of the locals say he was brilliant. I haven't been able to locate anyone by that name."

"*The Necronomicon* still, Robert?" I sighed, but Robert's speech was increasing in speed. I couldn't get a word in. He was barely pausing for a breath, let alone enough to hear what I'd said.

"But there was apparently a local artist named Pickman[1] who possessed a copy before his disappearance."

My stomach began to turn.

"I found a local man who was able to provide me with an incomplete copy of the Latin version of the book—on loan. It will have to do for the moment. He told me about a man in California who is purported to possess one of the only known Greek copies. Perhaps by comparing the two..."

"Robert," my stomach began to turn, "Who lent you a copy of the book?"

He looked at me for only a moment. "A gentleman out of Ipswich, John. I hardly see what that matters. Though something very strange is occurring out here in the Miskatonic Valley. Lots of cover ups. The man told me nearby Innsmouth was the

---

1   See note 1 from the prologue, pages 6-7.

subject of an investigation."

This was even more concerning.

"Robert, I think..." but Robert continued on, nothing seemed to be getting through.

"I've a lot of work to do, John," said Robert, walking off and not even looking in my direction. "Wish me luck. I'll show these stuffy old fogies what Robert Phillips can achieve."

V

Within a week following mid-term exams, Robert's bizarre behaviour went on seemingly unchanged with perhaps one exception: he rarely left his room, even at night. The fact that he was still awake at odd hours was notable by the soft light radiating from the window of his room on the third floor of the dormitory. Those coming from a late visit to the library or stumbling home from some off campus revelry were won't to note, even when others' lights were out, Robert was quite literally still burning the midnight candle.

Whatever he was up to, everyone speculated, and his reclusive nature was certainly no help to him in this regard. Many recalled the incident—witnessed or heard about secondhand—with Professor Rice, and they postulated about the true meaning behind the scene. Those who knew Robert, especially his closest friends, still had faith in him, even if they found the incident with Rice quite startling and surprising. They believed he was onto some terrific discovery. How little they, or even I, knew how terrific it truly was. All that I was concerned about was the safety and sanity of my friend.

After about three weeks had passed and I'd seen and heard nothing of Robert beyond the speculations of those around me, I decided to pay him a visit. I was growing increasingly concerned about Robert's mental condition leading up to and following his interaction with Professor Rice, and all that had seemingly occurred since his habits became more and more reclusive.

I had terrible feelings with concern to the nameless gentlemen in nearby Ipswich and out in my native California. At the time it was not so much the nature of their work or the dreaded *Necronomicon* itself, but because of the effect all of this was seeming to have on Robert and his studies. Were it not for what I believed to be his increasingly unstable condition, I might have otherwise thought little of the whole business.

Despite Robert's ability to take his exams and pass them (though well below what would otherwise be his expected performance), we could all see whatever Robert was up to was grossly changing the young and brilliant man we knew. Though I of course knew much more of what was happening to him, even if I was yet wholly ignorant of the deeper implications of his terrible obsession, yet I spoke of none of it to anyone. I wish I had not been so young and foolish then. Perhaps Robert could have been saved.

When I arrived at Robert's door it was sometime in the middle of the afternoon. Classes were going on, and I decided it was the best time to visit as fewer people would be around. It's the only time I can recall purposely missing a class in my entire academic career.

I knocked and there was no answer, not even a stir, and I wondered that he were not out and had perhaps attended that day's sessions. After a pause, I decided he might be sleeping and knocked again, and again, and once more. I was fit to start banging on the door just to be certain when suddenly it opened wide.

That man who stood before me did not quite look like the Robert I knew of even two weeks ago, and that image had been a mere shadow of his former self.

Robert was dressed in clothes that looked almost stiffened from sweat and soil, and with it came a rank stench as of unwashed flesh and rotten food. There was a staleness in the air, as though whatever the smell were made up of had sat incubating in the room for days. The form beneath the clothes was drawn, thin, and pale in colour, even having a tinge of green to the skin. The eyes were sunken, bloodshot, and hardly open, ringed with purple-black swelling. His chin looked as though it hadn't had a shave in a week. A groan came from the dry throat of the wraith before me.

"John," he said little else, and were it not for that, I would have hardly believed he was awake. I stepped into the room, despite the pungent, invisible wall.

The room was piled with papers, half eaten food, and blankets. Half burned candles lined the edge of the desk before the window. On the armchair he had beside the bed was a stack of books. The bed was piled with clothing no less worn and sticky than that which he presently wore. And the smell!

"Open a window, Robert, please," said I as I walked toward the window and threw back the curtains. Robert covered his eyes as the sun flashed through. I opened the window to draw in some of the cool, fresh November air. "Have you never left your room since exams?"

"Not entirely, John. No." I think he was too worn-out to respond very well to me. He looked as though all he wanted to do was to curl up on the bed.

"Could you at least tell me what is going on?"

He swayed about the room for a minute and than handed me an envelope. I saw the address was from California. Inside was a handwritten letter and attached four typed pages in what I recognised to be Greek. I looked up at Robert. He must have read the expression on my face for he presently spoke.

"He wouldn't send me the book, but he was kind enough to type out four pages of the Greek version for me to compare to the Latin version I've borrowed—on the condition I send him a perfect copy of any of my findings. I've already written him to send more."

I did not speak. I only listened.

"He seems quite excited about my ambitious plan to make a truer translation of *The Necronomicon*, but he states that he is uncertain of any Arabic version of the book. His, he believes, is the only Greek copy in existence. He assures me there are others who would be quite interested in my work and feels that there is no finer candidate than a man of my connexions to the Miskatonic Valley."

I paused, looking back at the letter, skimming it briefly. Nothing I saw in my quick glance was in contradiction to Robert's words.

"And what were your findings?" Robert sighed and sat down on the bed, hanging his head.

"Nothing conclusive, but it is quite possible

that Alhazred's original name was closer to Abdallah Zahr-ad-Din[1]. I've not looked into it much, but what I did find in the translations between the Greek and Latin versions are some startling inconsistencies.

"From the Greek to the Latin version, it seems Ole Worm needed interpret the meaning of many of the Greek passages."

"Ole Worm? Olaus Wormius translated *The Necronomicon* into Latin?"

This at least piqued my interest. I had at least a passing knowledge of the multi-talented old Dane.

"Of that I can't be certain. The dates don't quite match up to the Danish physician's lifetime[2]. But then what? Were the dates recorded wrong? Or is the name an odd coincidence and a pseudonym?"

"That's not known to be a common practice in the Middle Ages," said I, my interest rising.

"No it isn't, John, but perhaps it was misappropriated to Wormius," continued Robert. He was beginning to talk fast again, though my present interest in the subject was keeping me from thinking too hard about the deplorable condition of my friend and his room. "And of Theodorus Philetas, the man who is said to have translated the Greek version from its original Arabic, I can find nothing.

---

1   This rendition of The Mad Arab's name was also purported by a writer by the name of L. Sprague de Camp, who had an amateur interest in the subject, and had a connexion with one of Robert Phillips's family members.

2   This is true. In what little can be corroborated about the history of *The Necronomicon*'s translations, Ole Worm was said to have translated the book into Latin in 1228. Olaus Wormius lived from 1588 – 1654.

So I cannot even ascertain the man's proficiency as a translator."

Despite his condition, the real Robert was coming through again.

"All I can tell for certain is Alhazred or Zahr-ad-Din or what have you was purposely vague in his writings, which would have further lent to translation errors. It appears Wormius didn't always know what to make of Philetas's words, comparing what little my friend in California has sent."

"So what do you plan to do?" I asked.

"I sent for more pages, a wider sampling if possible. I plan to translate those and write a formal paper and request to the college. If I can prove the translation errors exist in the Latin version, they'll have to allow me a look at the book. And then imagine, John, I might make a name for myself even before the end of my academic career: Robert Phillips' new translation of *The Necronomicon* of Abdallah Zahr-ad-Din, and a whole new area of Middle Eastern history will be open to study."

With this Robert turned toward the window and stared out. I could see there was a look of passionate determination in Robert's eyes, and with it a strange unsettling mania which turned my stomach.

VI

What next occurred in this long unfortunate tale was the incident that was most heartbreaking for me.

For some weeks still Robert was absent from classes, and though I had given my compliance to leave him be whilst he finished putting together his findings for the college, I was never quite comfortable with the idea. There was something about the whole business I did not like. Not the mysterious man in California. Not the local man in Ipswich. Not even Robert himself whose habits and behaviour were becoming less and less recognisable to everyone who'd known him.

Still, I loved him. His was the best mind I had ever known, and I still hold that to be true. That is why I took it almost as hard as Robert himself for what happened next.

End of term exams were approaching yet again, and Robert at last began to appear on campus. He looked nothing at all as he had the past two times I had seen him. Robert once more presented as amiable, well-groomed, and as carefree as he always had. This too conjured up a slight discomfort in the back of my mind, but I did not give it too much voice. I was so happy to see my best friend back to his old self.

I didn't even bother to question him about *The*

Necronomicon or the man in California, and neither did Robert bring it up. He seemed entirely focused on two things: studying for exams and enjoying the time with his friends. It was only afterward, when I was able to give it more thought, that I realised there was something almost forced and unnatural about Robert's behaviour during that time. He laughed just a little too hard. He had just a bit too much energy. Every now and then there came into his eyes a look that I couldn't quite place—one that reminded me of the people in the asylum where my uncle had stayed until his death.

Then I recall, Robert stayed after our last exam, Etymology, to talk to Professor Rice. Ashton and the boys were going out for a celebratory pint and Robert assured us he would catch up in a short while. I noted that Robert was carrying with him a large bundle of neatly stacked papers. A chill stole up my spine when I saw them, and it was then that I noted Robert did not look as healthy and vibrant as I had supposed. I tried to stay behind. He insisted I go along with the others.

For the afternoon and into the early evening I remained uneasy, watching the door and catching my breath every time it opened, hoping Robert would walk through. The others, deep in their merrymaking hardly noticed Robert was even missing or that I seemed to be less enthusiastic than the rest of our party. At some point I said my goodbyes, and despite the pleading cries of my drunken friends, I wouldn't stay. All I could think about was Robert and what had occurred.

When I returned to campus, I found him in his room. He did not answer to my knocking, but I heard him mumbling to himself and the faint, regular sound of furious footfalls on the wood floor within. When I opened the door, Robert did not raise his eyes toward me, but I saw they were red and raw with tears.

"They burned the whole thing, John!"

"What do you mean, Robert? What happened?"

"The papers, John!" Robert screamed so loud I thought they'd hear him in the pub five blocks away, "all the work I did! Armitage snatched it right out of my hand and threw it in the fireplace!"

I shrank back from the sudden burst of rage, and carefully, shaking, I sat down on the bed, watching wide-eyed as Robert paced furiously and moved his hands about in violent gestures.

"I've been asked to vacate the campus once exams are finished. They're putting me on probation. They laughed at me! They threatened me! Me, who could write circles around them! Would you believe that?!"

My stomach began to turn. Again I found myself at a loss and merely sat watching the maniacal behaviour of an unwell man. I began to wonder if Robert hadn't acted like this in all of his encounters with the faculty over *The Necronomicon.*

"Something is being covered up, John. Or I'm being singled out. My entire academic career is going to be stifled by a small circle of jealous and greedy dotards! This is retribution for my genius! They're afraid to allow me to upstage them and bring prestige back to this university after they plummeted it into the ground! How dare they! I'll show them!"

His rant continued on for some time in a string of irrational and unconnected thoughts. I wanted to cry to see him in such a condition, and I didn't know what to do for him. All I could do was sit there and listen to it, stiff and afraid. He pacing and ranting, seemingly without pause or any hint of exhaustion.

At length, Robert stopped. It was sudden. He threw the pile of books off of his armchair in a last explosion of rage, and then he sat down in it and covered his face with his hands. A moment's pause stretched out to infinity, and I held my breath, purpling around the face and neck as Robert let out two long, heavy sighs.

"Let me be, John," said Robert and there was a weariness in his voice at last. "I need to think or do something to get my mind off of this. I'll be fine. I promise."

Without a word, I rose from the bed and walked out, looking back over my shoulder at my friend seated in the chair. Robert did not look up. He did not even move. He looked to me exhausted, despondent, and embarrassed. I knew he was sorry, though he did not say it. Indeed I only once more ever received an apology from him.

My head was spinning. With tears in my eyes, I made my way back to my own room and fell at once asleep.

Within a few days, I was packed and prepared to leave for the Winter Holiday. It had been a while since I had been home to see my parents in California, and it seemed everyone was going to leave Arkham for a bit, even those who lived nearby.

I invited Robert to go with me, but he declined. The mood which I had seen him in a few days before had passed. He was talking and acting like normal again. As I said, he never apologised this time, but I chalked it up to severe embarrassment at just how much he had lost control.

I asked him what he'd planned for the time off. He was uncharacteristically vague, merely stating that he was going to move back into his family's mansion and spend a bit of down time there and in the Miskatonic area. I dared not ask about *The Necronomicon* for fear it would anger him—especially if he had decided at the last to let the thing go. I was not so sure and his seeming secretiveness about his plans was not putting me anymore at ease.

If Robert was planning to continue to look into Alhazred's book, he said nothing of it. Had I known what was next to occur, I would have stayed in Arkham, even if my father was on his death bed. But I did not, despite my misgivings. Like the many times I should have done something to get Robert help, the fact that I left for California that winter after Robert's last major outburst is one of the biggest regrets I have in my entire relationship with the man. What I would do to go back.

VII

Out in California, I forgot about my studies for a while. I had decided to take a complete respite from anything to do with history or the economics thereof for as long as I was visiting my family. Though many times I thought of Robert and wondered how he was getting on. I sent a Christmas card (he had given me the address of his parents' mansion), but nothing came in return. After two weeks had passed, I wrote him a considerably long letter, telling him of how things were out West and asked explicitly for news about himself. But like the Christmas card, that letter also went unanswered.

I tried to dismiss it as likely that Robert decided to take something of a vacation himself and wasn't home to receive the letter. At least, I hoped that was the case. Yet as the days passed, despite the speed of the post from one side of the country to the other, I couldn't help but have an uneasy feeling about the whole business.

During that last week in California I was so entirely preoccupied with thoughts and concerns over Robert, and I was anxious to return to Arkham to be certain that everything was all right. All the train ride back I was a nervous wreck. As I passed from one state to the other, drawing ever closer to Massachusetts, I could feel my heart racing and I felt ill.

I arrived very late on a Friday night. There wasn't much snow on the ground, and it felt good to be around the old buildings of Arkham. However, because of the hour, I went right to the dormitory to lie down for the night, thinking to seek out Robert or any information about him as soon as I woke the next day. I did not have to go very far to find out what Robert had been up to over the Winter Holiday and why it was my letter was never answered.

It was all about campus that on Christmas Day, a security guard came upon a man trying to break into the restricted section of the Miskatonic University. Thankfully, the man had not succeeded and had even been captured. The security guard chased him off and in the pursuit, the burglar had taken a spill on some ice. The security guard could not identify the man, but supposed he was a student, on account of the gentleman's age and dress. So Dr. Armitage was called in as well as the police, and so it was Armitage who positively identified the burglar as Robert Phillips.

With Armitage at the scene, and in light of Robert's recent behaviour on campus, the University decided to press charges. Robert had been arrested, thrown in jail, and whilst there, expelled permanently from Miskatonic University. His name was smeared in the local papers and on campus alike. Other than that, there was no word about or from Robert, and no one was even quite certain if he was still in jail or not.

Within weeks of the term beginning nearly everyone who had ever been a friend to Robert or even known him casually was claiming they had always thought the man was quite strange and that there was something sinister about him. Even Ashton said that he was only friends with Robert because he had felt quite sorry for such a lost and deranged individual.

I made only a few attempts to locate him, at first, but the police would give me no further information beyond his arrest. I sent letters to his home—all without response. At some point, I merely gave up the idea that I'd ever see Robert again, thinking perhaps too that he had no desire to see me. That was the hardest part, as there was no one in the world I wanted to see so much as Robert and to be sure he was safe.

And so I was left alone to grieve Robert's loss, and buried myself in my studies to help stay the pain. Many nights, tears were in my eyes wondering what had happened to Robert, and if there was not something I should have done to stop this. I was the one who had seen the obsession growing and the deterioration of his mind for months, and I'd done nothing to help him or guide him away from his mad fixations and delusions.

I suppose I could be comforted in the fact that at the time I had only a version of the truth of what was truly happening to Robert—if I can even say now, all these years later, that I know anything for certain. Still I cannot help but feel that, back then, so early on in the whole affair, I might have been able to stop Robert from what I can all but prove was his ultimate fate.

But at the time of his expulsion, and for many years afterwards, I merely believed Robert Phillips, the greatest mind I had ever met, suffered from a serious ailment of the mind, and now would have no further academic career. I hadn't a single friend I could turn to to speak about it. I do regret not standing up for my friend in the years that followed, but I felt entirely alone and was afraid I'd lose what little friendships I now had.

Though in truth I hadn't much use for any of my peers or professors any longer, even Dr. Ashley whom I had so greatly admired, as even he was not above the occasional reference to the school's greatest embarrassment: Robert Phillips. I did not even like walking about the city as I used, though I had been always so taken with the old architecture of Arkham. Most of the time, like Robert had for that last year or so, though certainly with more care for myself, I spent in my room or in the library.

I worked hard and graduated with high marks, but nothing every quite felt the same after Robert was gone. Once I was done and graduated, I left Arkham, though I had formerly considered a seat in the history department at Miskatonic. I returned to the city again twice only after that. As for Robert, I believe I saw him only one other time alive or whole on this Earth, and in my remaining years at Miskatonic, I never once heard the least rumour about his whereabouts at the time.

Part II: Letters from Arkham

As I stated in my prelude to all of this, I will offer no conjecture as to events and actions which I cannot confirm and wish to offer only the barest possible statement of the facts as they were. I have never been able to uncover all of the facts about Robert's whereabouts between his expulsion from Miskatonic University and the next time I heard from him. Certain of Robert's claims I have since corroborated, but there is about a years' worth of time which is quite vague and will likely forever remain without explanation.

I have my own conjectures and fears, and you yourself, reader, may arrive at your own conclusions. I would say not to think too deeply about those conclusions, as often the mind creates a worse scenario than is actually the truth. Then again, never was such the case with Robert, and whatever your wildest imaginations, I would suggest the truth is likely far, far worse.

I

Somewhat fortunately, I did not have to go very far to find placement in a university as a professor of history. I'd applied to nearly every college in Massachusetts, New Hampshire, and Vermont. Thankfully, Harvard in Cambridge had need of a new professor, and I was able to begin what I had high hopes to be a long and illustrious, even if humble, academic career as a professor of Ancient History, and perhaps publish even a few books on the subject.

Alas that never happened, and this poor, unfortunate tale may be the only contribution I can make to Man's understanding of history and the universe.

By August 1937 I had relocated to a small room on Harvard's campus for new faculty and was already hard at work on research, creating my lessons, and matching my syllabus with the college's requirements. Then of course there were my own studies, as I could not be expected to simply sit on a chair in the college and not continue my own work.

Thankfully, I was so busy with work that I rarely thought about Arkham, Miskatonic, or Robert—though occasionally my mind would fall on him. It was always the same concerns as before: how he was doing; what he was up to. As the years passed, I was becoming more and more resolved that I might never know, and that was too difficult to bear. My own successes didn't make the fact any easier knowing that Robert was so much more capable than I (and of course not thinking myself incapable by a long shot).

Once the term began I found myself obsessively inspired by the environment at Harvard, and I thought of little else but classes, lectures, and my own modest studies. When not lecturing or studying myself, I'd discuss things with my fellow peers, or begin to learn the unfamiliar avenues of Cambridge and Boston next door, taking in the architectural history there. Even my family in California I rarely wrote to.

For the purposes of detailing the passage of time, I'll merely state that my first year as a professor went surprisingly well. Perhaps it was my single-minded focus on my work. The Summer was particularly difficult. I didn't quite know what to do with myself, though I had made many friends on staff and one or two locally in the City in that time, but there was still a sense of loneliness which I inherently knew only Robert could cure. That made things difficult indeed, so I threw myself into work and research again, trying my best to forget about what would likely never come to pass.

It was after the exams of the first semester of the following school year (that is, 1938 – 1939) that I came home to my little apartment and found a piece of mail waiting for me. The snow had made a mess of the envelope. Indeed it was a wonder that the postman could even decipher my address, but I could clearly see that the address of the sender was in Arkham, Massachusetts.

I cannot quite describe the sensation that came over me. It was equal parts excitement and dread, like as though a lightning bolt ran through me, surging with energy, and in a moment the energy passed away, and I felt as though I would be sick.

With shaking hand, I opened the door to my modest apartment and didn't even bother to take off my coat or put the kettle on for tea. I sat down in my armchair and opened the letter straight away.

Inside was a Christmas card which had written on it the simple phrase: "With apologies for its lateness, R. P." And with the card was a brief letter...[1]


```
                                       Letter #1
                            13 September 1938


Professor J. Lewis,


Congratulations, my dear old friend!
     I always had faith you would succeed
in becoming a stuffy old professor at a
stuffy old institution. But I do not
mean to diminish my praise. In all
earnestness, I am happy for you.
```

---

1   As stated in note 3 of the prologue (page 9), Professor Lewis included all letters separately and referred to them in his text by date and number. (He numbered them by hand.) Here was written "And with the card was a brief letter (see letter #1 dated 13 September 1938)." For the remainder of this publication, the publisher will merely cut off the reference to the letters as written by Prof. Lewis so as to offer a more seamless reading experience. Instead, the date and number of the letter will be inserted following its redacted reference.

I know it has been quite a long time. (Six years! How the time flies!) There is so much to discuss and catch up on. It took me a while to track you down, once I was out, but I have become much better at locating hidden things over the past two years.

I hope you do not find this letter strange. To be honest, I'd kept myself from sending it for a long time as I wasn't quite certain you'd wish to hear from me. I have bumped into one or two of the old boys over the past two years, and I cannot say they were at all pleased to see me. It would seem they've written me off entirely. But then I remembered you were different from the others, John. My one true friend, even through all the difficult times at Miskatonic and my many outbursts. I hope I am right in that.

I find myself in a strange place. Obviously my prestigious ambitions were crushed with the decisions made at Miskatonic, but I've been well at work on some things. I hear Llanfer took over for Armitage some years ago. But I shouldn't say too much. I'm not even certain you'll find this letter welcome. I hope you do. I haven't many friends left, it seems. Not from my old life.

I do hope you're well.

Yours,
Robert Phillips

Verily my heart broke to read of Robert in such a pitiable state. I imagined him sitting alone in his parents' solemn old home in Arkham. To think Robert would be without a person in the world when he had enjoyed so many friends whilst at Miskatonic was almost impossible. It was so easy for me to recall the best times with Robert, and to forget about what happened to him, especially at the end.

I read over the letter two more times, both happy that I was hearing from Robert at last and upset for the facts of Robert's present life. Then when I'd had some tea and time to let it gestate, I sat down to write him in return. Despite my feelings of melancholy, I attempted to put on my best face. I wrote to Robert requesting that perhaps we get together—after all I was on Holiday until late January—and made some general inquiries about what he had been and presently was up to[2]. There was a curious tone in parts of Robert's letter, something of an ambiguous foreboding. Though I did not hope too much that Robert had at the last given up his obsession with the dreaded work of The Mad Arab Abdul Alhazred.

It was not two weeks later that the response came...

---

2   Again, as stated in note 3 in the prologue (page 9), the publisher is not in possession of the letters of Professor John Lewis, and it would seem Prof. Lewis kept no carbon copies of his own. It will have to do that we take him at his word, and considering much of the evidence which can be corroborated in this book, as well as the responses of Robert Phillips, the publisher stands by the testimony of Prof. Lewis's reporting of his own words.

Letter #2
3 January 1939

John,

Happy New Years'!

I hope the cold isn't hitting you too hard this Winter. We've had quite a lot of snow out here in Arkham, and I find I am often too weary from long hours of work to clear it away from the front of my parents' old place. Thankfully there had been minimal damage here during the September storm[3].

    I do however sense a tone of concern in your letter (if I read it correctly). Please do not worry overmuch about me, John. I know you care. You were always the sort to see the best in people, especially me—even at times when I didn't deserve it—but know that I'm well.

    Whatever hardships have hit me are in the past now. Sometimes one must fail in their endeavours before a big breakthrough. I can say for certain,

---

3   Here Robert must be referring to the Great New England Hurricane which caused immense damage in New York, New Jersey, and all of New England in late September 1938. Even Canada was affected, though considerably less so by the time the storm reached that far north. Curiously, Prof. Lewis does not mention it in his manuscript, but Harvard was the owner and maintainer of forests which were wiped out entirely by this storm.

John, that I am making good progress
now and understand so much more. Much
time was lost while I was away, but I
have had much luck and success since.

    I don't want to say too much right
now. There are a few other things to
complete, so I have to decline the offer
to meet. Perhaps once you've finished
out the second term of the school year.
By then I should have quite a lot to
show you.

                          Your Friend,
                            Robert

I can't say that Robert's second letter was entirely
settling to my concerns about my old friend, but
at least his words sounded sane (how I hate to
put it like that). I wrote him back at once, hoping
frequent letters from me might help cure Robert's
loneliness. Though in the end it seemed there was
little purpose to my letter. I had only put it in the
mail but two days before and was preparing for the
opening lectures of my courses when I received a
call from the Arkham police.

II

The call from the Akrham police was from an Officer Hawthorne on behalf of one Robert Phillips.
The request was that I, the only known friend or
acquaintance of Mr. Phillips that could be gotten
a hold of, and he having no known living family,
make the trip out to Arkham to post bail for Mr.
Phillips and to pick him up from the station and
take him home.

If he could not post bail, the officer continued,
he would be detained until his initial court appearance which would be scheduled for six months
hence. I attempted to ask what this was all about,
but Hawthorne was rather short and was off the
phone quickly. So, with still about two weeks remaining before the term, I packed a few things,
and went to the bank to get a check for the amount
of Robert's bail. Fortunately, I'd always been rather
frugal with my money and had the sum available.

With the snow, the drive down was not the most
convenient. It took some three or so hours to reach
Arkham, and that was two days after the call from
the police. As I approached the city, my stomach
turned.

Notably many of the old buildings were in a
ruined or half-fixed state, and even a couple of
the avenues were closed off. The Great Storm had

done quite a bit of damage down there. Though the effect of it all, with the snow falling, trees hanging from buildings, and great gaping holes in roofs or even some walls that were still remarkably left standing, had the look of a decaying corpse. I felt a dreadful foreboding as I drove up to the police station, and I recalled one of the lines Robert had spoken of from the Mad Arab's tome:

That is not dead which can eternal lie.
And with strange aeons, even death may die.

It sent a chill up my spine, and I half imagined that I saw the anthropomorphic creatures sketched in that book Robert had found in New York were peaking out from the broken windows of the many abandoned homes and buildings: winged, gelatinous-skinned abominations, with hideously tentacled faces and large, wet, bulbous eyes. Certainly this was the sort of land they would inhabit, had they existed. The insane conjurations of a lunatic mind, yet they haunted me all the same.

By the time I reached the police station, I had a curious sense of foreboding. I was kept waiting about an hour whilst the policemen moved about the station and my paperwork was processed and payment validated—a simple call to the bank. I sat on a bench working on some notes to improve the term's lectures, and at some point, lost in my work, I heard a familiar voice:
"John."
I looked up and there before me was my old friend, much changed in the years since I last saw

him.

His hair was already flecked with white, despite his youthful age, and there was considerably less of it than before, especially for a man of his mid-twenties. Though you could not have guessed his age, as his face bore evidence of great care and weariness, adding ten or twenty years to him. He had a beard too, which only in his worst condition I ever recalled Robert growing.

His frame to was much too thin for such a young man, when vigour should have been at its height. Though most frightening of all were his eyes. Where once they had been brilliant blue, they now looked dull and grey. I would have thought him blind were it not that he recognised me from afar.

But when he smiled, in that one moment, it seemed he hadn't changed one bit, and despite the shock of seeing the shell of the man I called my friend standing before me, I could not help but smile.

The car ride to the old Phillips mansion was not as amicable, if you will. We had a slow go of it as the snow began to pick up once more. I did not ask any questions. I tried to give Robert the respect of telling me about whatever it was had happened in his own time, but my heart raced to know exactly what had occurred.

"Thankfully Llanfer was much more lenient than Armitage," were his first words after some silence had passed between us. Robert was merely staring ahead into the falling snow, but it seemed as though he did not see it. His eyes were wide. Manic. Again, I kept silent and let Robert talk, but the thumping feeling in my chest did not subside.

"Though it appears I'll have to go back to court. A small price to pay for the knowledge I now have."

There was a silence again. Robert continued to stare ahead, and when I looked at him I suddenly had the sinking feeling that he was not at all well. His skin even seemed to have something of a greenish hue to it, which I vaguely recalled noticing once or twice in the past.

"Three years in Arkham Sanitarium," Robert spoke again. "Three years I spent in that Hell hole because of Armitage's paranoia and jealousy of me." My heart sank into my stomach at those words. I felt as though I were going to wretch. "He kept visiting, you know? Making certain I didn't get out as he believed I was a harm to myself and others.

"I had to keep any talk of Alhazred or *The Necronomicon* secret except to one man alone. Simon. He took great delight in my work. Armitage testified that I had paranoid delusions concerning the book and was obsessed with it. I don't want to be thrown back in there, John. It was a nightmare place, you know?"

I had never told Robert about my uncle, and I did not get into it then either. Merely I replied, "Yes, I have visited one in the past." Even though at that moment a great empathy for my friend entered my heart, my stomach still churned as though filled with acid.

"I was right, John. There are translation errors in the book, and even the copy here in Arkham is not without them." Now Robert finally blinked and turned away from the windshield and looked at me. "I am not insane, John, though Armitage tried to paint me that way. He is such a fool. I have learned there are hidden truths in the Mad Arab's words. I've lost so much time because of him.

"But I am now nearing the end of my work, and thanks to some friends. Hopefully the old man is still alive when the acclaim hits. I plan to mail him a copy when I'm done. He'll probably drop dead when he sees it."

Strange now that I know how right Robert was in assuming that, though not for the reasons he believed. Thankfully Armitage died before Robert's work was completed. I may now know that there is no God, or anything resembling a force for good in this world or beyond it, but at least fortune granted Armitage that for his own horrible experiences. Would that I had been granted the same, and saved from all that I know.

For the short remainder of the drive to Phillips Manor, Robert continued to stare out the windshield with a wide, unblinking stare, and my heart broke to see it. He almost seemed unaware that we had arrived at his home, and I had to call it to his attention. Robert didn't even blink, but looked down, opened the door, and rather stiffly got out of the car, almost as though in a trance. When I myself had gotten out and rounded the car, his demeanour seemed to have changed. He was smiling again.

"Do you have the time to come in for a bit, John?"

I smiled back, but at that moment, I hadn't the inner strength to do much more. Silently and obediently followed him up the stairs.

I had never been to the Phillips Manor, but I would imagine in happier, less decrepit times it was a majestic place, one which old Protestant sensibilities mixed with the innovative minds of the New World. What stood before me, however, was the abyssal mockery of that majesty. The spires stood out like horns, and the broken windows like the empty sockets of a skull. The roof had a massive hole in it, where a great tree branch had caved it in like an Indian's axe to the head. Robert had done nothing to maintain the home or fix it up since the storm in the Fall.

Without a word about the condition of the place, he opened the front door.

As with the outer appearance of the place, inside Phillips Manor was a wreck. There were no lights or candles in the entrance hall, but for the moonlight streaming from the windows and a hole somewhere above. It seemed also that Robert did little in the way of heating the place for the air was as chill as it was outside.

He led me into a room off to the right. There at least there was some evidence of life, though it reminded me heavily of the condition of Robert's room at Miskatonic University the last time I visited it all those years ago.

Clothes were strewn about. Crumbs and long rotted and stale food mixed with garbage, books, and papers. The fireplace at least looked like it had been in regular use, and one of the couches was made up in a makeshift bed.

"I've taken to spending most of my time here," said Robert, idly dismissing my obvious look of concern. "The mansion is just too big for a bachelor."

"Robert..." I barely whispered, and then my eyes caught the coffee table and the book and papers laid out thereon. The book was unmarked, save for obvious age and wear from multiple readings. It was unrecognisable to me, but on the papers beside it were written the words that I had long ago read when Robert first began his obsession: *Ph'nglui mglw'nafh Cthulhu R'lyeh wgah'nagl fhtagn* and their English translation, as Robert rendered it: *Cthulhu dreams awaiting his call from his home in lost R'lyeh.*

"The work is nearly done, John," said Robert. "After I had gotten out, I made straight for California, but my friend there died in a fire, and his copy of *Al-Azif* with it. I returned to Arkham, lost and uncertain, but then I was told of a distant cousin of mine, a Ward Phillips[1], living in Rhode Island and writing under various pen names, no doubt to protect himself, who knew about the book intimately.

"Quite an imagination he had. He passed away last year. This book here he hid from all, but I was visited some months ago by a strange man name Barlowe who said he was a friend of Simon, and that Ward's book was to pass to me. He also added that there were many who were greatly interested in a true translation of *Al-Azif.*

"I can see why. I'm afraid Ward was not much of a linguist, even if he were a fine writer. Look here, John. That strange language, he translated this line as: *In his house at R'lyeh, dead Cthulhu waits*

---

1   All evidence suggests that Ward Phillips of Providence, Rhode Island wrote under many pen names over the years including Lewis Theobald, Humphrey Littlewit, and H. P. Lovecraft. Records indicate that he died in March 1937, and some of his personal papers and books were indeed lost and have yet to be found.

dreaming. But R'lyeh is referred to elsewhere as the nightmare corpse-city. "Dead" refers to R'lyeh not Cthulhu, and it is too literal a translation of the word from—" But I couldn't listen to much more. My fears had gotten the better of me at the last, and I cut him off.

"Enough, Robert. This is too much. This obsession is killing you! Just look at you. You're not right, Robert. Surely you must see that?"

Robert stiffened, and he looked upon me coldly.

"I thought you were my friend..." he whispered barely audibly.

"I am, Robert. I hate to see you like this. Please. Let's go to the hospi—" I barely got he words out. Robert's eyes widened, and he came at me as though to hit me, his teeth bared, arms flailing.

"I'm not going back there, John! I'm not insane! Don't you see what's happening here?!"

I could not, not in whatever sense Robert meant, and dear God I wish I had listened to him then instead of judging. I tear up just to think of how I might have saved him had I chosen a different course. But my mind was swimming with fear, and I backed away from the unrecognisable Robert Phillips, toward the front door.

"Get out, John! Get out! And I'll be sure to mail you a copy too when my greatness is revealed to the world, and I expose this lie of the Miskatonic University! Get out!"

His voice was rising to a shriek, near to deafening. Frightened I ran to the car, Robert still screaming incoherently. Without looking back, I left Arkham and headed straight for Cambridge. It was an hour into the return drive when, grown man though I am, I broke down into tears.

III

It was too difficult to even think of Robert and that last encounter between the two of us. I seemed numb to it and fell into working with renewed focus and a single-mindedness that had not before existed. Reality, it appeared, was far too difficult for me at the moment, and I preferred the company of the long-dead men of the past. The new term began, and I seemed unbothered by any real troubles at all. But like most emotions stuffed and hidden away, they're always right there, ready to resurface. The catalyst was a new letter from Robert.

Falling back into our old familiar pattern it seems, Robert's letter was apologetic in nature (see Letter #3, 16 February 1939[1]). He stated frankly that his nerves were shot from long hours of translation work, and the fact that his new-found friends, Simon and Barlowe, were often and anxiously checking in about progress with the translation. He ended again with his sincerest apologies for his behaviour, and that he still held my friendship above all other relationships in his life.

Despite my injured feelings, I was not at all angry with Robert for his outburst and hastily wrote him a letter in reply so as to not keep him waiting

---

1 This letter is quite short and the publisher has opted not to include it here, especially as professor Lewis explains its contents quite accurately.

in dreadful silence for a response. I expressed that no apologies were necessary, but that my only concern was for him, and that out of love of friendship I would support him, so long as he promised to take care of himself first and foremost.

Indeed, this is not to say I was not deeply concerned for Robert's well-being, his mental and physical state, and his very life, but I could see quite clearly any direct approach to addressing this with him was only going to yield resistance. So I decided to remain in contact with him and give support from afar (that is until I could make it out to Arkham again). Then perhaps a serious intervention would be done or at least I could persuade him to see, over time, the pitiable condition this seeming untreated ailment of the mind had reduced him to.

Over the course of the Spring term Robert and I wrote frequently back and forth—and Robert often sending two letters for every one I sent him. Despite my intentions, it seemed I was having little to no affect on Robert's condition or his obsession. Indeed, it seemed my correspondence with him was only encouraging his behaviour and any subtle attempts to get him to see the facts of his reality went unnoticed.

More, his letters became more alarming in nature in such a relatively short time. Over the course of three months, Robert it seemed had very nearly finished his translation work, and had been paid a visit twice by the strange man named Barlowe who had given him the book of his Cousin Ward. Only once did Simon accompany him. These visits seemed to have a strangely unnerving effect on Robert, though he did not express any direct feeling of concern or apprehension. I could only deduce this from his words, as you might yourself in Letters #5, #6, #9 and #11[2].

It seemed that he had an affection toward Simon, but Barlowe on the other hand, though Robert was indeed indebted to him for the copy of his cousin's Arabic version of *The Necronomicon*, did not put Robert at all at ease. And I could certainly see why. He described Barlowe as an awkward fellow, seemingly alien, and quite obviously a foreigner. Yet Robert could not place it. He described Barlowe's mannerisms as strange and almost stilted, like "the movements of a puppet under the hand of an amateur puppeteer"[3]. He almost never blinked, and his body seemed "off somehow, though it's difficult to say how"[4]. Robert also described a strange accent

---

2   Due to rising paper costs, the publisher has decided not to include transcriptions of Letters #3 – 11*, and especially with the author describing the important details of the otherwise pedantic correspondence (see also note 1 above). Again, the publisher asserts that Prof. Lewis's description of the nature and content of these letters are completely accurate, and little else of relevance needs to be conveyed to the reader.

*[2019 Publisher's Note: This note, as well as all others contained herein, appeared in the original 1943 edition of this book. Since its first publication, all of the papers of Professor John Lewis have been lost. The present publisher thus regretfully cannot reproduce these letters.]

3   These are Robert Phillips's exact words, highlighted and included by Prof. Lewis. From Letter #6, 20 February 1939.

4   Ibid.

and a poor command of the English language.

Again nothing specifically unsettling about the man, but Robert seemed to be fixated on these little oddities. I thought nothing of them at all at the time, but now I am convinced of the hideous truth of this Barlowe.

Also evident in the letters, Robert's attention seemed to be increasingly turned to the very content of the book itself. As he translated it, he became ever more enamoured with the concepts laid out therein, stating things such as: "can you believe it, John? A whole group of entities inconceivable to the human mind? What if our entire race's concept of God and the Universe is completely inaccurate? What if al-Hazrah's[5] book is the key to the truth?"[6] and "The ascension of humanity to its truest form. To make contact with one of the Great Old Ones."[7].

No doubt this was the influence of Simon especially, but Barlowe as well. I did not like those two, but knew if I came down too hard on the subject, Robert would likely become defensive. I hoped he would come to realise it on his own, but in his state of mind, I saw that these men were having a strong influence on my previously reasonable friend. And then came the letter of 4 May:

------

5   By this point in Robert Phillip's work, he was apparently using Abd-al-Hazrah as a translation of Abdul Alhazred in keeping with the Islamic mystic traditions of Sufism and conforming more nearly to Arabic usage.

6   From Letter #7, 23 March 1939.

7   From Letter #9, 3 April 1939.

                              Letter #12
                              4 May 1939

My Loyal John,

I'm due in court in three days hence,
and I know Barlowe and Simon will return
for news on the book. I've insisted on
including the[8] section on the translation
history of *The Necronomicon* [sic][9]. It
is only fitting I trace it as accurately
as possible in order to stake my claim
on the inaccuracies of the original
English translations and my own more

---

8   Phillips's use of the word "the" here is correct.
He referred to this idea in three other letters previously.

9   Though Mr. Phillips was sometimes still using the title, *The Necronomicon*, he always wrote it followed by the notation as shown above. It is apparent
also from Phillips's letters that he was vehemently in
disagreement with the translation of the book's title as
The Necronomicon, but was being forced to maintain its
usage by his patrons, the mysterious Messers. Barlowe
and Simon, in order to not confuse any future readers. It is also apparent by Mr. Phillips's words that he
was going to be allowed to make his case for a new,
more proper title for the book in his Introduction to the
translated text, though whatever that was, along with
Phillips's alleged introduction, has been lost. Likewise,
the name Abdul Alhazred still appears to be the most
accepted printing of the Mad Arab's name, though in
any Arabic translations in which his name appears it
is rendered as Abdullah Alha zred (based on the scant
research the publisher has conducted on the matter in
order to better stand behind Prof. Lewis's testimony).

accurate, contemporary translation.

But I've hit something of a wall. I've been going over and over again the impossible words of Abd-al-Hazrah. They intoxicate me, as do the finest lines of Homer once did in my youth, yet they conjure a vigour which I have never before felt. There is truth in them, John. There has to be. And to hear Simon's and even Barlowe's descriptions of things they've seen through al-Hazrah's work. I have never so been drawn to a man of the past's work as this one.

It would seem a pity, wouldn't it, that I should do all of this work for them and not reap any of the benefits thereof? That I should not know the truth of al-Hazrah's words before even they?

There is a small thing I might attempt. I feel compelled to. I'll write you back again if it appears to have worked, else, please just dismiss this as idle fancy.

Yours,
Robert

I was not to dismiss it as "idle fancy", however, and with the increasingly unstable words of my friend, I was set to leave for Arkham as soon as the term ended. I wrote Robert a calm note in return referring in a supportive way to his most recent claims.

Even now I feel guilt for the deception, but I assert I was only doing it for his own good. Only, it was to no avail. Nothing further I did was able to change the course of things, and I never received a direct response to that letter or the two others I sent after it, and I was unable to leave for Arkham for the entirety of the Summer holiday.

IV

The life of a dedicated and competent college professor (if I may be so bold) is not without its obli-
gations and at times, inconveniences. Before the
Spring term had ended, I was approached by the
head of the department to join him in some very
important research work for the University, which
would require travel. Harvard was to pay for the
whole thing, and my name was being put forth as
a most reliable and promising mind in the field. In
fact, I had the full support of the upper faculty. It
was the chance of a lifetime.

I nearly went white when the news came to me,
however, and it was supposed by the head of the
History department, who came to me directly, that
it was the shock of happiness. But in fact all my
thoughts were on Robert and how he might do in
this time of obvious crisis. I tried to plead my case,
but the department head at first dismissed me,
insisting there was no one in whom he had more
confidence than I. But as I tried to make my case,
his complements slowly turned to criticisms. So in
short, out of fear and confusion, I chose poorly and
took the job as requested (might I say demanded?)
by the University.

Over a month in Greece would have been a joy for
me under better circumstances, and I do regret

that I was not able to enjoy the trip or the work. I did my best to keep up all pretense to the contrary, especially as now I was on official business and in representation of the good institution, but my mind was constantly racing with thoughts of Robert. Now I was even further from him, and the response times would be slower. I could not even hope to give him any assistance now and only prayed that business would not extend the entire Summer, that I might make a trip out to Arkham before the Fall term.

My mail was being successfully forwarded to my address in Greece. I still received letters from my family. But no word came from Robert whatsoever. As I stated, I wrote two more letters to my friend, from Greece, and nothing came back to me. Then, it was near the very end of our trip, and the beginning of August, that I received a letter from my mother that my father had fallen terribly ill and were not possible to come out to California to see him as immediately as possible. Everyone was understanding, and there wasn't much left of the work, so I went straight out to California and did not return to Cambridge until the 30th of August.

The college was more than accommodating in the wake of my father's passing, on account of all of the good work I'd been doing, including with the long project in Greece. But as soon as I'd arrived back, having buried my father and settling my mother in with relatives as comfortably as was possible, and with the promise of returning for Christmas, I was of course expected to begin teaching with the beginning of the term.

My brain was in a fog at the time. The only glimmer of happiness was a letter that sat waiting for me from Robert. Apparently, as I later learned, the letter was sent out to Greece but arrived just after my early and sudden departure. The college then rerouted it back to my place in Cambridge, and there it remained, with a second letter which had arrived only a few days following the first.

Letter #13
2 July 1939

My Good John,

Sorry to have startled you with a lack of response. I'm certain you must have been worried (as if I haven't worried you enough). This may sound silly to you, but I attempted some rituals as described in *Al-Azif*, first from my English translation and then was going to use the original Arabic as my guide, before the interruption.

I could not help myself. Unfortunately, I wasn't very good at covering the whole thing up. I'd rather not go into details, but the police were phoned and arrived at the manor whilst I was in the process of the Arabic version. As I was already due in court in two days, I was taken in.

Court went fine. I was ordered to pay a heavy fine for my transgressions, in addition to an order that I not go within an hundred feet of the college again. Barlowe and Simon will no doubt reimburse me for it, but the real turn was having to go back to the Sanitarium.

Between the strange lights that were reported to the police, and the fact that my break in at Miskatonic involved *The Necronomicon* [sic] again, despite Llanfer's leniency, the judge wanted me evaluated again. Another three weeks of being poked, prodded, questioned, and observed. But I've been through this before and had a much easier time giving the doctors the answers they wanted to hear. I gave them no reason to keep me this time whatever.

I am home again and plan to make another attempt at the ritual. I wasn't quite able to finish, but based on the way it was going, I fear I may have made an error in my translation work. I confessed this to Barlowe and Simon. They were none too happy for the fact, but agreed to give me more time all the same.

I wonder if they know what I'm up to?

Yours,
Robert

And as if that were not alarming enough, the second read as such:

Letter #14
7 July 1939

John,

I had to take a few days to calm my nerves. I certainly was right about my errors in the translation.

It's remarkable, yet frightening what occurred. What appeared before me as though a vision. The Nameless City as it once was. Sunken R'lyeh. The impossible titterrings of the Old Ones. Can it really be true?

But the sensations that followed. Could this be what killed my cousin? I have a theory on that, John. But I dare not write too much. At some point Barlowe and Simon are sure to catch on that I've been sending you letters. They won't be pleased. This was all a risk, but it couldn't be helped. The desire was too great.

First Armitage and now these two. This is my destiny, John! My destiny! Miskatonic is in my blood, and the words of Abd-al-Hazrah speak to me from ages past.

I will be the first!

Robert

My stomach turned as I read those final words. I could not help but feel Robert was becoming completely unhinged. I am ashamed to say I felt his words so impossibly delusional that I began to doubt the characters of Barlowe and Simon were indeed real.

I was in a pickle. What was I to do? The term was starting. My job would have been on the line, and already I had tested the head of the History department's patience on the subject of my "ailing friend in Arkham" before we went to Greece. If it weren't for my mother's letter, I'm not so certain he would have believed me about my father after that.

So I wrote to Robert directly, expressing my sincerest concern for his well-being. I encouraged him to phone the authorities concerning these men, Barlowe and Simon. If they did exist, they were thugs no doubt, and the police were more capable than I of dealing with them. If not, Robert would be committed again, for his own good. I also let him know the facts about my whereabouts for the past months and about my father. Our letters must have crossed in the mail, for I received this one but a week to the day after sending mine.

Letter #15
28 August 1939

John,

I hope nothing horrible has happened to you, and please say that you have not abandoned me, dear friend.

Barlowe and Simon and have been to see me twice. They grow suspicious—even

Simon. I assured them that I am trying to make a definitive translation of the work (as such as any man may), and that it has come to my attention that there are inconsistencies in my work, which is the complete truth. They must believe that much for who cannot read sincerity in words spoken honestly?

I know now for certain my Cousin Ward was merely a slave to them, working to spread the word of their unnameable cult of Yog-Sothoth worshipers. They say Ward died pitiably and alone. Did I tell you that Barlowe claims to have a journal from the man's last days, and all that he experienced?[1] Ward had something of a voracious interest in history and science.

Cancer they said. But I think Ward tried the book for himself and that is what led to his end. That's why they sought me out, and I was already willing. Perhaps I won't give it to them after all.

Oh, the Eldritch knowledge which will be imparted to me, John. And you too! For do not think I would leave you out, so loyal a friend have you

---

1   Other sources reference and confirm that the "death journal" of Ward Phillips did exist and was lost. Alleged re-printings of certain excerpts from the journal are available to the inquisitive mind, but if Mr. Robert Phillips and Prof. John Lewis's accounts are to be believed, it is likely theses excerpts are passable forgeries perhaps created by Barlowe himself.

been. Then we might indeed visit the
Ancient lands of Egypt and Greece as
they were—and far more Ancient lands
still!

      I've almost worked it out, John.
Abd-al-Hazrah was a clever man. Too
clever. For he was in fear of the Great
Old Ones, but I believe there was no
reason to fear. I think I can work out
the cypher he used. I plan to attempt
again in a few days.

                              Robert

My mind raced over Robert's words. He was completely falling apart. That was evident. But the new
term was beginning. I don't know how I got through
it all. Never mind that letters began coming from
California stating that my mother was in a severe
state of melancholy. I'm told that during those beginning weeks of the new term I shook visibly and
nothing more that came from Robert did anything
to calm my nerves.

V

The next letter arrived swiftly following the likely arrival of my response to letters #13 and #14. I dared not confuse the situation more by sending a follow up to #15, though it was taking all of my inner strength not to rush off to Arkham unannounced and without any notice to the University.

<pre>
                              Letter #16
                         5 September 1939

John,

I'm so sorry to hear about your father.
Please take care of yourself and your
family first.
     I can't say much now. Don't write
back. Just wait for some word from me.

                              Robert
</pre>

There was no return address on the letter this time, as if the letter itself was not disconcerting enough. It was almost too much to comprehend. I could barely handle the confusion of it all. And letters were coming from my mother which were equally, though very differently, tinged with the tone of instability. I wrote to my mother, taught my classes, and after a day or two of ruminating over what to do, I phoned the police station in Arkham.

Likely I sounded nearly as hysterical as my mother and Robert seemed to be of late. I was deathly afraid that Robert had gotten involved with unsavoury persons, and that in his condition, they were attempting to manipulate and control him. It was difficult, but I was ready to believe that Robert was much more ill than I had ever before imagined. Untreated, he was only deteriorating further.

The man on the phone seemed none-too-pleased about sending men out to check the Phillips residence. No doubt they'd had quite enough of Robert at this point. But I'm certain knowing his history and hearing the concern in my voice, they obliged to check in on the man and see if he were all right. If there were anything to be concerned about, they would ring me back at the college. I'm not so certain they even checked, especially in light of the next letter I received from Robert.

Letter #17
21 September 1939

John,

I've had to vacate the old mansion and have come out to Innsmouth to finish my work.

Barlowe has become threatening, and Simon is not the friend I thought he was. They do not understand that I have truly arrived at an accurate translation of the book, but I'm having to begin much of the work again from scratch. I need the quiet and the seclusion.

Much of the town has been abandoned for years now, and the people here have a strange look to them. Somehow they remind me of Barlowe. I can't explain it. There's a sea-like quality about them. Their skin seems perpetually wet. Their eyes bulge, and they slouch and shamble mindlessly whenever I catch one of them walking about town—which is not often.

I'm afraid you can't write me here. I'm having to secret these letters out, and if anything comes in, no doubt Barlowe and Simon will be able to locate me.

I can't let them have the translation, at least not until I've finished it and learned the truth for myself. Perhaps not ever.

Wish me luck, John. I nearly made contact this last time. I'm certain I'll be successful now.

Robert

My hands shook as I read the letter over again and again. Just what was happening to Robert? I'd long had a theory that Robert suffered from an ailment of the mind which I only knew vaguely as Manic Depression. He seemed to have exhibited what few symptoms I knew of. Now my dear friend was out moving around in a paranoid state to keep away from these real or imagined men who purportedly wanted his accurate translation of a book of Eldritch, cultish knowledge written by a man whose own moniker was "Mad".

I nearly cried to think of the man Robert might have been were it not for the unfair circumstances of his birth. Was I harsh in judging him so? Even now I cannot be certain that Robert did not suffer from some ailment of the mind. But was it mental illness that made him more susceptible? Or was it the twisted obsession with the mad scrawlings of a man who had delved too deeply into the abyss and saw the unnameable realities which existed just beyond the reach of our human and flawed vision? Perhaps it was some combination of the two which made Robert such an apt candidate for what happened to him.

When his next letter came, I became deathly afraid that Robert's diagnosis, so far as I was able to ascertain it, was in fact Schizophrenia (which is what my uncle had suffered from). I panicked with the fear that he was a danger to himself and others.

Letter #18
3 October 1939

My God, John, what have I done! But how can I say that? There can be no God, not while such things exist.

Horrible. Unnameable. And the sounds. The awful titterring and buzzing.

The horrible, gutteral mockeries of human speech. The scratchings in the night, and the impossible shapes I've seen silhouetted in the dark.

John. Abd-al-Hazrah. Abdul Alhazred. The Mad Arab. He was right. All he wrote and more is true. Cthulhu. Yog-Sothtoth. The sunken corpse city of R'lyeh. I have seen for myself only a fraction of the mind-numbing Eldritch truth.

It is too terrible. We are but a spit-stain upon the world. Unremarkable to things beyond our knowledge. Yet they know now that I know of them. Ward found himself in such a place, and he died for it. Alhazred the same. That must be why he coded his words, that men might learn the truth, glean it, but never reach so far.

It is beyond comprehension, John, and they do not wish us to know even the least bit about it. I will die alone and in obscurity.

Barlowe and Simon want the book, but I cannot in good faith to my fellow man ever give them this translation. Armitage was right to refuse my access to this thing years ago. Whatever happened, whoever that Whateley was, Armitage must have known. I still recall the cold sweat on his clammy face when I first asked about the book.

Oh, John! They are searching for me. I must leave Innsmouth. I dare not

come out to Cambridge or go back to
Arkham. I don't know where to go.
        Don't write me. I won't be here.

                                    Robert

I fell sick immediately upon reading the letter and
canceled all of my classes for the remainder of the
week. I swooned in a fever for three days. I was weak
and pale and barely had the strength to fix a meal
or tea. Thankfully one of the other professors was
kind enough to check in on me. The staff at least
knew about my mother, and believed my nerves
had at last broke. They insisted I do everything I
could to remain calm through the end of the Fall
term, even to give me assistance if I so needed it,
and then to take a sabbatical for the Spring term.
        When I woke feeling mostly refreshed on
Sunday, there was a letter beside my bed. It had
arrived on Friday, but I had been too ill to notice it.
With a shaking hand I took it up and opened the
letter to read:

                                    Letter #19
                                    undated

Please, John! Come at once! I need your
help! I cannot bear this alone, and I
don't know what else to do. I'm at this
address in Salem. I'll remain here.
Hurry!

                                            R

With a shaking hands and tears in my eyes, I slowly attempted to get up from the bed, but my legs were far too weak. The fever returned. I did not wake again until late Monday morning.

VI

After some rest, I planned to go at once to the head
of the department and ask if they might find me a
suitable replacement for the remainder of the term.
I had to find Robert. I did not even know if I would
find him at the address on the letter.

I was still weak from the illness brought on by
my frayed nerves, but well enough to move about
again. I shaved, dressed, and was about to walk
out at last in the evening when I saw that the post
had arrived for me that day, and with it was another letter from Robert. Mind you, I will state here
that it was that day 16 October.

```
                                      Letter #20
                                 13 October 1939


My Dearest Good Friend, John Lewis,


How are you, sir?
     I write to tell you I am well-
minded, John, and have taken your good
and honest advice to seek a doctor.
I am now with him. He is taking good
watch of me.
     Do not worry dearest good friend,
John. I will be a good and fine man of
```

```
normal ways again, once the doctor has
done with me.
      Patience, friend John. I will write
to you again.
```

```
                        Good and Healthy,
                        Robert Phillips
```

I knew so little about more recent psychiatric treatments and the effects they had on the mind of the mentally ill, but I knew there had to be some altering effects. I recalled that much about my uncle. Certainly Robert's letter was considerably calmer than those which he had been writing to me of late, but was so uncharacteristically like him. At the time, I wondered if he was not undergoing some severe electroshock treatment or being given insulin to sedate him. That might have explained the very strange nature of his letter. How wrong indeed I truly was.

For that time, I believed my good friend to have finally, by force or by his own resignation to the fact, gotten the help he so desperately seemed to need. Indeed, until the very last incident, that damnably mind-numbing thing I must believe I saw that night in the Phillips Manor, I believed this to be the case entirely.

If Robert's letter was to be believed, then I could at last stop worrying about him—at least as much as I had been. He had gotten himself help, or at least someone had taken him to get it. Either way, he was in the care of a doctor. Would that I had been more discerning and suspicious. Would that I had believed so much more than I did. But all I saw was a suffering friend, and I wanted to believe that his nightmare was finally over.

My nerves calmed. I was able to concentrate on my work again. Even my mother's difficulties were not producing the same shaking weakness I had been experiencing for weeks. Though I was very anxious to hear from Robert and know that he was doing all right, I trusted to the belief that he was finally going to be fine.

I imagined often what it would be like to see him again, well and like his old self. Perhaps some of his good qualities would be gone, but that was alright with me. As long as he was happy and healthy. Then perhaps he really would achieve that greatness I believed it was his destiny to obtain.

October went by with excited expectancy. It was just into November when Robert's next letter arrived.

```
                              Letter #21
                          2 November 1939


Dear John,


I am deepestly sorry for all the problems
I have put you through, and if any of
my recent writings have upset you.
     I am well, and there is no need
for you to worry over me anymore. It
is very apparent that I have been the
victim of a sickness of the brain, one
which has caused me to be abnormal in
my behaviour. I am sorry. I have made
```

a big mess. I am sorry. You are a good friend, and I am happy you are mine.

It was so hard to do, but I decided to look for a doctor, and I found one that could help. He took me back to Arkham where I have been under the supervision of a Dr. Jacobi.

He demands I take rest and not upset my brain. Please do not write yet. I will write to you again in fourteen days to let you know I am good and no metamorphosis has happened.

I will write again. Please promise me my wishes.

Friend of Yours,
Robert

Believe it or not, I sighed with relief to read that letter, and I felt he was at least sounding calm and reasonable. Then, almost on the very day two weeks later, another letter arrived. It was the very last I would receive from anyone by the name of Robert Phillips.

Letter #22
11 November 1939

Dearest John,

I have needed the time for rest, and the time is over. Dr. Jacobi talks that I am making the best progress, and I am

```
happy.  I  would  very  much  like  to  see
you.  I  want  to  describe  my  sick  brain
to  you  and  why  it  is  that  way.  I  also
want  you  to  look  at  me  so  that  you
can  witness  that  I  am  the  same  Robert
Phillips  that  you  have  always  known.
     Please  come  see  me,  John.  I  can
explain  everything  and  make  your  brain
as  calm  and  happy  as  mine.  When  you
arrive,  come  at  once.  The  time  does  not
mean  anything.


                              Love,
                              Robert
```

I was honestly delighted to read this. I believed this trip could finally ease my concerns, and so I hastily wrote a reply that as soon as the term was ended I would be on the first train out to Arkham. As it was, I still had classes to teach, exams to give, and papers to collect and grade. If all truly was well with Robert, I saw no reason to be in any haste. Oh! But would that I had not gone at all and had been mercifully spared the horror I believe I witnessed that final night and of the horrid implications thereof.

VII

It was then two days after the end of the Fall term when I left Cambridge for Arkham for the very last time. Never again have I returned to that horrid place, and unless I am taken there by force, I remain resolute in my decision to avoid it, as you shall soon understand.

Though that night has haunted my every waking and dreaming moment since, I will muster the strength to give as detailed an account of the events as possible, so as not to leave out a single fact.

The air was oppressively cold that December and a frigid wind blew which would have chilled even the most warmly dressed person's spine. This time I went by train, having no need for a car. I arrived late on the night of 20 December at the Boston Maine Station, and it was a miserable walk to the French Hill district.

There had yet been no snow that year, and despite many of the repairs from the Great Storm of the previous year the landscape looked like a veritable decaying waste. Even though I looked with hope to the prospect of seeing my old friend again, I could not help but be effected by the sinister quality of the town at night in the dead of winter. Perhaps I was somehow in tune to the blasphemies which lurked and likely still lurk there in the Miskatonic Valley.

As I approached Phillips Manor, my stomach gave one final turn that night. Veritably, from the outside the mansion looked no better than it had a year before. The same broken windows and the same great hole in the roof. Surely in a month's or more's time Robert would have had the ability to have the place fixed up a bit. Certainly the good Dr. Jacobi would have insisted on it.

A strange foreboding came over me at that moment, and I wondered that it was not a fear that Robert was no better off than he had previously been, but in fact worse now, and his manic psychosis had reached its peak. Even more disheartening, I could not see the faintest glimmer of light from the windows. I was so cold and tired.

Despite this and recalling Robert's wishes that I go to Phillips Manor as soon as I arrived, I was not deterred. I still held onto hope that I would see my old friend in his old state. Though admittedly, I was so exhausted that I planned to have a short conversation with Robert and save the rest for the morning. Robert no doubt would be tired as well, I thought.

However, when I knocked upon the door, the faint glimmer of matches being struck and candles being lit filtered through the windows to either side of the front door, and soon I was face to face with a silhouetted form in the door. I cannot quite describe what precisely it was, but I had a strange feeling when looking upon it. Something about the form seemed off. Though the shape was generally Robert's, the posture wasn't right somehow. Then came the strained though familiar voice of Robert Phillips.

"John. You came."

The light was so dim I could not see a smile or much of his face. My heart sunk for just a moment, thinking that whatever the doctor had done to my friend, though it stablised him, it left him much changed. Still I smiled back.

"Hello, Robert," I said. "Yes. And it's good to see you."

He extended a hand rather awkwardly and I took it. The hand even did not feel right. The grip was stiff yet without much strength. His skin felt loose somehow, as like an old man's whose muscles didn't hold him together as they used. Another change and another disappointment. Though the shock was so great upon touching his hand, I had to keep myself from recoiling in horror. I did not want to upset Robert. He was well now, whatever change there might be. I had to believe it was for the best.

Once inside, my eyes adjusted to the faint, warm light of the candles, and I began to see Robert fully now. He was dressed not in a robe as for bed, but in a fine suit the like of which it had always been his habit to wear in our youth. Nothing of his old disheveled appearance remained. His face was cleanly shaven, and I daresay his skin looked healthy, even if a bit pale. Though he'd lost more of his hair and was slightly bent, he looked more the Robert I had known during our years as students than I had seen for too long a time.

His speech too seemed much the same, save that on occasion, he might stumble over a word or pause at strange times as though he had forgotten the word he wished to use. But even this I didn't find so strange, attributing it to the symptoms of a still recuperating mind. However, save for the dim light alone, there was only one thing which I found to be entirely unnerving. Robert's eyes.

It was not their colour, for indeed their old blue brilliance had returned. Rather they seemed unnaturally wide and did not often blink. There was a glassy quality to them as though he were under some form of hypnosis. Much like the times I saw him at his worst over the years. I wondered that he would not always stare like that. It was difficult to look at him, I'm ashamed to say.

"I apologise for the poor lighting, John," said Robert. "I have...lived in the dark for so many years now, my eyes are not quite...used to bright lights yet."

"That's quite all right, Robert," I tried to reassure him. I didn't want him to feel the least bit awkward now. "I can see just fine." And after a slight pause, with another smile I said, "it's so good to see you, man."

"Yes," was all the response I got as Robert led me into the room off to the right, the one that had previously been his sole living quarters.

As I stated, the outside of the mansion was still in the same state it had been when last I visited, but the entrance hall had been respectably cleaned up. Even more so, when we entered the living room, I saw that it was much improved. Gone were all the rubbish and papers, and the furniture looked as though they were being used for their conventional purposes. That at least gave me some cause for relief. Whatever the doctor had done, it was having a positive effect, it seemed. I sat down on one of the couches which had previously been occupied by books and clothing, and Robert sat across from me on the one which had formerly been his bed. I supposed now he had a proper room set up elsewhere in the mansion. I looked down at the coffee table. Much to my relief, there wasn't a single book. No *Necronomicon* or otherwise.

I will not trouble the reader with overly pedestrian details. I can recall the conversation, word for word, that night with stunning clarity, especially considering what followed. Let it suffice that Robert and I first spoke of my own work, my mother, my father's death, and my trip to Greece. Robert nodded much through the conversation, and his responses to verbal and visual cues seemed awkward. Still I my only suspicion was that Robert was adjusting to his new-found health. As we got on in the conversation, Robert smiled more and more, and he asked more questions.

Following my tale, he explained that he was suffering from a severe form of schizophrenia—or at least that is what Dr. Jacobi believed—but that the doctor was ill-equipped to assist Robert any further. It was his strong recommendation that he leave Akrham and the Miskatonic Valley behind him permanently.

"Dr. Jacobi thinks it will be...best for me, John," said Robert. "...Apparently...my psychoses are strongly connected with this place. He believes a new...location...home will be best for my condition. That's...somewhat...why I called you here. This is goodbye, John, I'm afraid, at least for...a while."

In that moment my heart broke one last time for Robert Phillips. I might never see my friend again, and indeed, I never did nor do I believe I ever will.

"Of course we...remain friends, John," said

Robert. "I can still write you...on occasion...but I need to leave my past behind me so that I can... heal further. Perhaps one day I can return to... America."

"Return?" I said with a quirk of my head. "Where will you go, Robert?"

"Dr. Jacobi's son is traveling to Italy. He suggested I go with him. With my...knowledge of... Latin, he thought I might do well there. Then, after many years, perhaps I can come back."

I nodded my head, and a silence passed between the two of us. It didn't feel the least awkward. It never did with Robert. I merely wanted what he was telling me to sink in.

Though I would miss my friend, I knew so little about ailments of the mind. I could not protest whatever the doctor was recommending. It seemed apparent from the beginning that this whole business with Alhazred and his mad book were a great source of mental stress for Robert. Perhaps life in a new location, unconnected to any of the history of *The Necronomicon* would be for the best. Perhaps in time he would be in good enough shape to come back to the United States. And I supposed there might also be the chance to visit him overseas at some point in time.

I had so many questions to ask, but it was late. I was still of the mind that I needed to be as supportive as possible of whatever course Robert wished to take. After all, I was about the only constant thing in his life. I did not wish to ruin that bond between us, so great was my love for him. So I braced up, swallowed my sadness, and slapped my knees with both hands.

"Well, Robert, that sounds wonderful! I'm certain you're going to be very happy, and you look so well already."

I smiled and Robert smiled back, but there was something stiff and unfeeling in the expression. I barely noticed it at the time, but thinking back, it brings chill up my spine. I rose from my seat and went to extend my hand out to Robert to congratulate him on his great success. Robert rose as well, and he somewhat awkwardly moved forward in the half-dark to meet me. And that's when the thing happened, that seemingly unremarkable moment that carried with it so many hideous truths that it nearly broke my mind.

It was the dull clunk of a glass falling upon the rug, preceded by the thump of my host's shin on the low table between us. I thought nothing at all of the sound at first, and rather went to Robert's aid, reaching out my hand to catch him. But even as I came forward, I saw that Robert groped frantically upon the floor for something. Then recalling the sound of glass, my eyes moved but inches from where his hand groped and fell upon the object which I knew then to have made that sound.

Seeing it, I let out a soft gasp, but not so low as to be unheard by the thing upon the floor. As the sound escaped my lips, my host turned its attention from the object it sought and looked me full in the face. At once I recoiled in horror and let out from my lungs a scream the like of which I have never before—and I hope never shall again—let out.

EPILOGUE

How I managed to cross into that hall, work the knob of the front door, and run inexhaustibly to the police station is a mystery even to me. Such was the terror evoked at what I saw—or rather did not see—in my host's face, that I was given to the most intense shaking, nausea, and dizziness. Even my speech was effected, so that when I arrived at the station I am told I was thought to be a gibbering lunatic. I was to be escorted to the Arkham Sanitarium myself were it not that, at the last, I fainted upon the lobby floor. I woke in St. Mary's Hospital in Arkham two days later.

After being examined by a doctor to confirm I was of sound mind, I was then questioned by the police as to what had me so hysterical as to barge into the police station in such a state and at such an hour that night. I did not speak to them of that final horror I had witnessed, nor of the unspeakable things which I had now come to guess for fear I might be thought insane.

I did tell them, however, of the things I suspected Robert to have done and which he all but confessed to in his mad pursuit of the knowledge of Alhazred. I spoke of the men Barlowe and Simon, and of Dr. Jacobi. The police at once went to the Phillips Manor, knowing already of Robert's history, but their search turned up little. No one was home. The place in fact seemed to be abandoned but for some objects left behind and a note, written in a curiously shaky hand, but signed *Robert Phillips*, stating in short all he had told me about his permanent relocation to Italy.

They did not find the translations of *The Necronomicon* Robert had made or the copies he had obtained of the abhorrent book. All evidence pointed to the fact that the man simply had, due to the long years of his sullied reputation in Arkham, up and left hoping to start anew elsewhere and not wishing to be found.

In the entire case there was only one fact that could never be confirmed. There was no asylum in the area which had any records of admitting a man named Robert Phillips, not since his last recorded and rather short stay in the Arkham Sanitarium that previous summer. More, no local hospital or asylum had a doctor on staff by the name of Jacobi. But the authorities dismissed these inconsistencies and let it be. No doubt even if they suspected Robert Phillips had gotten in a bad way, they were glad to be rid of him.

Following those events, I left my post at Harvard with little explanation. I never did see my mother alive again. I was told she died four days after Christmas, and likely from heartbreak that I did not keep my promise. My life ended that last night when I visited the Phillips Manor, and since then I've had single-minded determination to find and destroy every possible copy of that dreaded book of the Mad Arab known as Abdul Alhazred.

Al-Azif. The Necronomicon. I know now that every coded and unspeakable blasphemy in that hideous book is true. The things that Alhazred saw, the visions of the Nameless City and of lost R'lyeh and the slumbering Great Old One, Cthulhu. I have since learned too that the Miskatonic Valley has been a center point of the cults worshiping the unnameable horrors described in that book. But followers of Dagon, Cthulhu, and Yog-Sothoth have spread. Whatever investigations were made into the happenings in Innsmouth in the 1920s and Dr. Armitage's own involvement with a man named Wilbur Whateley were for naught. (I never had the chance to speak with Armitage before he passed away.)

The cults may be dormant now, but their reach is spreading. That much is evident by Robert's findings in New York and California and the copies of *The Necronomicon* that exist in many of the world's most prestigious library colleges. And the man Simon and whatever it is that thing calling itself Barlowe truly was. Even now Barlowe hunts me for he knows I know the truth, and he knows I am attempting to destroy Robert's work.

Please, if you are reading this, I beg that you believe what I have confessed and confided here. The task is too great for a single man, and the emissaries of the Great Old Ones grow nearer with every passing day, despite my nomadic existence. My inheritance is nearly dried up, my friends vanished or they have cut me off. I write this only that I might make a wider effort to stop whatever damnable thing these crazed fiends hope to accomplish.

If you find a copy of a book called *The Necronomicon,* destroy it at once! Do not read it, for it will drive you to a mad obsession and a horrible

end. Think of what I have told you of Robert Phillips. I pray that I do not meet the same end as he.
I will blow my brains out before the cultists take
me if need be.

I know that the thing that wrote those final letters to me was not Robert Phillips. Robert's last
letter was that strange panic-stricken note which
had sent me from Salem[1]. Would that I had rushed
to his aid, but what good would have come of it?

I could never have gotten there in time. Even if
I had, I would likely have suffered the same fate as
my friend.

Oh! What cruel, unnameable things were done
to him? Was he even alive anymore in any sense of
the word? No. How could he be? I have seen the
crude illustrations of those unnameable things. I
have read their descriptions. I saw those horrible
depictions in the books that Robert read and in
that pamphlet in New York. But none of that can
compare to the horrors of the real thing.

I looked into the face of that thing that night
in Phillips Manor, and what I saw in its eye was
enough for a lifetime of insane nightmares. For
verily the object which fell upon the floor that
night was one of the petrified eyes which had once
belonged to Robert Phillips. And when the thing
looked up at me I saw the black, gelatinous orb
which gave sight to the nameless amorphous horror who walked in Robert's flesh!

---

1   Letter #19, undated; page 92.